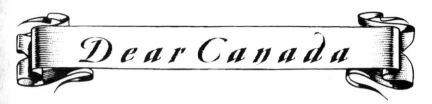

ALL FALL DOWN

THE LANDSLIDE DIARY OF ABBY ROBERTS

BY JEAN LITTLE

Scholastic Canada Ltd.

Montreal, Quebec, 1902

Friday, June 13, 1902

This morning my father was killed.

Even though I have written this down in black and white, I cannot believe it.

Father was such a strong man. He was a master stonemason and proud of his iron-hard muscles. Whenever he challenged John and his friends to an arm wrestle, they didn't stand a chance.

But when the scaffolding he was standing on collapsed and sent him plunging headfirst to the ground, his strength could not save him. They say he died instantly.

Later

That is not what I thought I would be writing in the notebook Miss Radcliffe gave me yesterday. She said it was because she knows I love to write, and in it I could tell the story of my summer.

I was looking forward to starting it tonight, but then we heard about Father.

I need to set it down.

It happened this afternoon while Mother and I were sitting in the kitchen peeling potatoes. I must have been singing to Davy when Father fell. Surely I ought to have felt the world stop turning for an instant. But I didn't. Instead I kept singing "Ring Around a Rosie." I would peel a potato and, when it came to the line "All fall DOWN!" I would toss it into the pot of cold water. When it splashed, Davy would hoot with laughter and I would start on the next one.

Mother was shaking her head at our nonsense when we heard running feet outside and our front door burst open.

It was Billy Brigson from up the street. He is usually a cheeky little boy with a big grin. But not this morning. He just stood there, staring at us, shaking and speechless.

We learned later that Billy had actually seen Father fall. Picturing him watching Father's head strike a granite boulder so hard that it split his skull makes me feel sick at my stomach. The horror of it was still there in Billy's wide eyes. In books, they say people go white as a sheet at such moments. Billy was grey.

"It was no place for a child," the foreman, Mr. Tyler, told us afterwards. That was why he had sent Billy hotfoot to break the news to Mother. Billy must have run like the wind. When he burst in and saw her smiling at him, though, he was struck dumb.

I can't go on writing. But I will be back. It keeps me from falling apart.

Still Later

I am ready for bed now, but I am sure I won't be able to go to sleep yet. The house is so still that I think I am the only one left awake.

When Miss Radcliffe gave me this notebook, she

never guessed that I would begin by telling of Father's death. I'll pick up where I left off.

When Billy didn't speak, I said, "What's up, Billy?"

But he didn't answer.

"Sit down, child, and catch your breath," Mother said quietly. "Then you can tell us what's amiss."

He sat down. He was still shaking.

Mother told me to get him a drink of water.

But something in the look on his face kept me rooted. Mother glanced at me, but before either of us could stir, words finally began to pour out of him. Davy was staring at him but he did not even notice.

"The men are coming," he babbled. "Mr. Tyler sent me to tell you. The scaffoldng tilted and Mr. Roberts fell. They're bringing his body. It happened so fast. He was a good man, missus. I am so sorry . . . "

A sob choked off his next words. Mother took his hand in hers and held on tight until he began to breathe more normally.

"Thank you, Billy," she said then. "Delivering bad news is hard, but you did nobly. Now please go back and tell them I will be ready for them."

Big tears were splashing down his cheeks by then, but he did what she said.

When the door closed, she reached out and took the paring knife from my fingers.

"Do not be afraid, Abby dear," she said quietly. "We will come through this. We'll hold onto each other."

"Yes," I said. I don't know exactly what I meant, but she astonished me by laughing and leaning forward to kiss my cheek.

"I always knew I couldn't do without you, Abby," she said. Her voice shook, but I heard each word. They puzzled me, though. Why would she ever have to do without me?

When Billy left, I heard Olivia beginning to practise the piece she is going to play at her recital next week. "Humoresque," it's called. Plainly, she had not heard Billy come and go. I thought Mother would send me in to get her, but instead she told me she was going up to change her dress so she would be ready when the men arrived. I was to stay with Davy until she came back down. Then she would break the news to Olivia while I went to tell John.

The very idea of having to deliver such a blow to John horrified me. He loved Father.

"Olivia should go," I blurted.

Mother had started up the stairs, but she turned and said, "No, Abby. It is your strength John will need. And I'll want Olivia's help here."

Before I could object, she was gone. When she came back down, she was wearing her Sunday dress and she started right in to explain what I was to do.

"Find Mr. Dunlop first and tell him why you have come," she said, "and then break the news to your brother and tell him to come right home."

The school is not far. I ran down the street, trying

to think what I would say. I wished it was over.

When I got there, I was startled to see John and Mr. Dunlop standing at the top of the front steps talking. I didn't stop to think. I just stared up at him and burst out, "John, Father is dead. The scaffolding collapsed and he fell. Mother said to tell you to come straight home."

He stared down at me and his face froze. It was like watching somebody get turned to stone. Then he pushed past Mr. Dunlop and ran for home.

Mr. Dunlop came down and patted my shoulder and said how sorry he was. I thanked him and followed John. Some inner voice told me what to do next and I obeyed. I was like one of those wind-up toys you get for Christmas. You turn the key and set it down and off it rattles. It doesn't stop until it runs into something. Davy loves those things.

It is late. Maybe I am tired enough to go to sleep now.

I just realized, for the first time, that this is Friday the thirteenth! How strange that I wrote the date down and did not even notice. I hope I never have another day like it.

This notebook is comforting. Nobody will pry into it, because it just looks like an ordinary school book. To me, it feels like a safe hiding place though. It is exactly the right size for keeping a record of my changed life.

Saturday, June 14, 1902

Putting things down this way steadies me. When Mother saw me writing in here, she said, "I've noticed that writing things down always helps you to get through bad times."

It's true, but I did not guess anyone knew but me.

I think I remember every single minute since Billy burst in yesterday. Yet none of it seems real. I wonder if acting in a play is like this. You would recite the words but not feel them. The outside of me did everything it was supposed to, but inside I just felt a stranger to myself.

When I reached home from fetching John, Mother told me Davy was napping. She said that when he woke up, she thought I should take him over to Miss Radcliffe's so he wouldn't be disturbed by all the coming and going. It's a good idea. He loves Miss Radcliffe and crowds do upset him.

Olivia was in the doorway, covering her face with her hands and sobbing. She has always been Father's pet. People kept patting her shoulder and doing their best to comfort her.

"Poor child," one of them said. "She did love her father so."

She did love him. It was true. But I knew my sister better than they did. I could tell she was enjoying showing everyone her broken heart.

"That's quite enough, Olivia," Mother said firmly.

"Crying won't help. Please go and put the kettle on and make a big pot of tea."

Olivia gave her a look that said Mother had no heart, but she went. I stayed in the corner where it was shadowy and waited to see if Mother needed me. But there was such a crowd around her that I felt I should just keep out of the way.

I stood there until my legs began to shake. Then I decided to come up here and sit with Davy. Climbing the stairs, I felt I might cry after all, but I did not. Davy would be upset if he saw me in tears. He's a happy little boy and seeing sadness in others worries him.

When he woke up, I changed him and gave him his bottle. Then I took him to my teacher's house. Miss Radcliffe played her parlour organ for him and sang silly songs. Davy loves music. He doesn't sing words, of course, but he hums. He sounds like a happy bumblebee.

When we went home, I learned that Father's body was in the spare bedroom upstairs. Mr. Stilson, the cabinet maker, and his helper will bring the coffin tomorrow and, after that, Father will lie in the front parlour until the funeral on Monday afternoon.

It was past suppertime but the house was still filled with people. It was a mystery to me how word had spread so fast, but later Mother said nothing travels as speedily as bad news.

John was mostly outside with the men. Olivia kept

crying in spite of Mother's telling her tears would not solve anything.

I did not have tears to hold back. Mother and I have always been close, but it was different with me and my father. He was proud of John and fond of Olivia, but Davy's slowness drove him mad. Sometimes Father would call him a lackwit or a simpleton and then wink at John and Olivia until they laughed. Mother and I pretended we had not heard. But when he said such cruel things, I hated him. I have never understood this, but I believe Father enjoyed being hurtful. When Mother grew angry at him, he laughed it off by saying, "The boy does not understand a word I say, so what is the harm?"

The harm was not in what his cruel words did to Davy but in the coldness in his voice when he spoke them.

I must try to forget this. It is not something I ought to remember.

After supper

Ever since we learned of Father's death, Mother has gone steadily on being brave. She told Mr. Stilson she wanted the casket closed.

People brought us more food than we could get through in a month of Sundays. The minister prayed over us. He used his preaching voice. It sounds syrupy and it always makes me squirm.

That is enough about this dreadful day. Nothing

has felt right since Billy Brigson burst through our front door. I feel numb inside. I could hardly wait to go to bed, but going would mean deserting Mother.

The funeral will be on Monday. If only it were over.

Saturday evening, June 14, 1902

Father's death has changed everything in our world. Right now I feel a need to keep track of how we will manage.

You hear people call their husband or father the Head of the House sometimes, and that is what Father was to us. He was not a comfortable sort of person, but he always knew what each of us should do and he checked up on us to be sure we had done it. Now he is gone, where will we turn? Perhaps writing things down will hold me steady, like an anchor keeps a ship from drifting out to sea.

I just read that over. It sounds highfalutin. But true.

Miss Radcliffe dropped by again this evening. She had found a storybook she thought I would like. It is called *What Katy Did*. She slipped it into my hand and said, "A good book can be a true friend at a time like this, Abby dear." Then she left as quickly as she'd come. She is so kind. I've stolen glances at the book already. Katy's mother is dead and her aunt cares for the children. I cannot bear to think of ever having to face life without Mother.

I wish I could just sit down and lose myself in the story, but of course, I can't. There's no place in the house where I could count on being alone, except in my room with Davy. If anyone saw me, they would think I was heartless. Am I?

After midnight

I can't sleep. Well, I did at first, but now I am awake and everyone else in the house is dead to the world.

How strange it is to write down that everyone is dead tonight, when Father is really dead downstairs.

I have been looking at Davy asleep and remembering when he was born. The doctor told them to put him in a Home and forget him. He said Davy would never be normal and probably not live long. He said that Mongoloid children rarely survive for more than a few months and that it was better for Mother not to let herself grow attached to him.

"You have healthy children. Concentrate on John and Olivia."

"And Abby," Mother said.

I was in the corner rocking Davy and I remember the doctor catching sight of me then. He looked flustered. "Of course," he muttered.

Father would have done what the doctor said, but Mother would have none of it. Lying there in bed, she looked weak and ill, but her voice snapped like a whiplash when she gave her answers.

"It is too late. I am already attached," she said. "Abby and I will care for him as long as he is with us."

Father said she was not strong enough, but she stuck to her guns and the two of us have tended him ever since. He was too much for her to handle alone, so even though I was supposed to go to school, Mother arranged to have her old teacher, Miss Radcliffe, who was retired and lived nearby, give me lessons at home.

Miss Radcliffe says I have writing talent. She is one of my favourite people.

Now I think I might sleep. I wonder what brought those memories to my mind tonight. I know really. It was thinking about Father's being gone and realizing that he'll never call Davy a lackwit again. I hated that so, and now it is over.

Sunday afternoon, June 15, 1902

We are waiting again. That is what we do most of the time these days. We wait and eat and thank people, and then wait and eat and get kissed and then wait and eat and listen to people tell us how sorry they are. It never ends. Worst of all is being patted and stroked and hugged and kissed by old ladies who are strangers to me. Their kisses are whiskery and sometimes their breath smells mildewed. I long to push them away, but Mother says I must be polite. I don't see why.

I hate them watching me when I'm tending Davy too. I love him dearly, but I don't enjoy taking care of him every minute of the day. And I hate being watched and cooed over while I do it, as though the two of us are not real but some sort of performance.

Abby, I cannot believe you just wrote those words! What is wrong with you?

I think I know. It makes me ashamed but I can write it down in my private notebook. I believe that, when the people are kissing me and staring into my face, they're trying to see if I have cried as much as Olivia. She has cried enough tears to fill a lake. Her eyes are all puffy and red. Does this really show how deep her grief is? My eyes are dry. Am I abnormal? I long to ask Mother about this, but she has enough to bear at the moment.

Snatching time to write in my notebook or read a page of *Katy* helps me to stop brooding about such idiotic thoughts.

After the funeral, I hope things will be ordinary again. I couldn't bear to go on feeling so lost.

Monday evening, June 16, 1902

We all went to the church for Father's funeral, all but Davy. He stayed next door with Mrs. Scott.

People kept telling us what a fine man our father was. I never knew what to answer. He took care of us, of course, but I don't think he enjoyed us. This sounds crazy, but he didn't know how to play. I wonder if Olivia remembers sitting on his lap when she was little, or being hugged by him. She was their first child. When she was born, he was still young and maybe happy to be the father of such a beautiful baby girl. I still cannot imagine him playing with her. I know I don't have any such memories.

Oh, Abby, forget it.

Tuesday, June 17, 1902

Billy Brigson was at the funeral. His hair was slicked down flat and he was wearing a suit and tie. He did not look like his usual self. I winked at him and he looked shocked. Father did like Billy. And Billy liked him too. I was thinking about this when some woman behind us said, "It's strange how little the younger girl resembles the rest of the family. Is she adopted?"

Somebody told her to lower her voice and Mother gave my hand a comforting squeeze. But she did not need to. I know I look different, but I like my face. Mother would have told me if I were adopted.

The others all have straight fair hair. John's is darker, Olivia's pale gold. I have to admit it is beautiful. And Davy's is almost as yellow as a baby chick. Their eyes are brown, but not the same shade. John's are nearly black and Davy's are tan. Olivia's are golden brown, of course.

My eyes are very bright blue. And my hair is an ordinary brown. It is curly on damp days. I have lots of freckles in summer. Long ago, when I was small, Grandpa told me he enjoyed looking at me because my funny face made him smile. It sounds insulting, but it wasn't. I felt as though he had given me a present.

Tonight, after supper, I was so sick of being sad that I took my skipping rope down the lane. I skipped to one hundred and fifteen without missing a step. I chanted a skipping rhyme and felt much better when I came home. And I felt wonderfully wicked.

I whistled too, very softly. Father forbade Olivia and me to whistle. "Whistling girls and crowing hens, Always come to bad ends," he would bark at me if he heard me. Olivia stopped doing it, but I like it. Also, I do it much better than either she or John. So I can't resist.

Olivia saw me skipping and looked scandalized, but I did not care. I wanted to tell her to try it herself.

Wednesday afternoon, June 18, 1902

I am writing while Davy naps. I am grateful to him. He sleeps a lot, which gives me an excuse for escaping upstairs. I can hardly believe how much I write. Downstairs there is always somebody wanting to sympathize. I've had all the sympathy I can stand. Maybe, when Davy wakes up, I'll take him and go visit Miss Radcliffe again. It would be a break from this house of grief and I could thank her for *What Katy Did.* I love it.

Later

I did take Davy to Miss Radcliffe's and we had a lovely few minutes. But I knew I shouldn't stay.

When we got home, Father's lawyer came to see

Mother. I believe there is more wrong than Father's dying. Mr. Burroughs spent ages with her. He closed the parlour door firmly and kept his voice low. After he left, she did not come out for ages and, when she did, she looked so tired I almost cried like Olivia.

She went straight to the kitchen and began bringing food to the table.

John asked her what the man had wanted but she shook her head.

"Not now, John," she said. "I cannot face another session about our problems. We'll talk tomorrow."

Nearly twelve o'clock

After everyone had gone to bed, I could not sleep again. So I crept down to get myself a drink of milk. I saw Mother through the open kitchen door. She had her head buried in her crossed arms and she was weeping. I almost ran to hug her, but then I didn't. She would not have wanted me to see her so distressed.

I forgot about getting milk and tiptoed away. When I was halfway up the stairs, a breeze blew in the landing window, bringing the sweet scent of roses. How can something be so lovely while everything else is terrible? There is so much about life that I do not understand.

Thursday, June 19, 1902

Today the minister took John to the hearing into Father's accident. When John came home, he looked years older. They had brought in a verdict of "No negligence." Mother had to explain this to us. It means that the company will not give Mother any money to help her pay the bills, because it was not their fault Father was killed that way.

But *he* did not make the scaffolding collapse. Billy told us that one of the supports had not been properly anchored. John wanted to ask whose fault it was then, but they did not let him speak.

None of the men looked at him, he told us. They said they were sorry and our father would be missed, but they never once looked him in the face. Mother asked Reverend Bricker what he thought of their decision.

"It is shameful, but I doubt you can get it changed," he said. He thinks the men will keep to their story and claim that Father must have tripped and caused the accident himself. They fear they will lose their jobs if they name the guilty party.

"The Brigson boy says he saw what happened," Reverend Bricker went on. "But nobody will accept the word of a child. I believe they plan to take up a collection to help you. But I doubt that anybody will officially admit responsibility. And once they give you whatever is offered, there won't be any more. We'll ask the congregation to help, but I fear that won't amount to much."

John lost his temper then and started pacing back and forth like a wild beast and shaking his fist in the air. But Mother told him it would do no good. She looked pale and weary, and the minister left after making a short prayer. I shut my eyes and tried to listen to him, but Reverend Bricker was muttering the words and hurrying. I could not take it in.

Later

I just remembered something puzzling that happened while all the people were here after the funeral. One of the ladies asked Mother if we had family we could turn to for support and Mother said, "Yes." I was amazed. I wanted to ask her who, but I couldn't. The lady would have expected me to know. What did Mother mean? I remember Grandpa, but he died when I was little. I had never heard of any other relations. I have kept meaning to ask, but there were always so many people around watching us and listening in when we talked to each other.

This afternoon, after we had finished eating, Mother told us what the lawyer had said. It turns out that Father was in debt when he died and left us next to no money. He was earning, of course, and had no idea he would not live into old age and pay back what he owed.

John stood up when she began and tramped up and down. It is hard to believe that Olivia is older than John — but then, she was only ten months old when he was born. But I suppose it's because more is expected of him since he's a boy.

I'm too tired to go on now. It was so surprising and so complicated after that. But I will tell it all tomorrow.

Bedtime

I don't want to have to tell all of what came next, but I'll try. It was so startling.

When John paced about, Mother watched him and I could see she felt sorry for him. But she was impatient too.

He wheeled to face her when she paused. "What did he spend it on?" he demanded, glaring at her, as though she, not Father, had wasted the money.

Mother kept her voice level and said that Father made investments which he thought would bring him a fortune, and he loaned money to friends in trouble. "Never mind, John," she said. "That is past and it won't help us to dwell on it. Right now we must make plans for the future."

"What future? How can we make plans with no money?" John shouted at her.

Mother drew in a deep breath, smiled at him and calmly announced that she had written to her brother Martin for help.

John sank down in the nearest chair and stared at her, open-mouthed. Olivia and I were just as stunned. None of us had ever heard of any uncle.

"You don't have a brother," John said uncertainly.

"Oh yes I do," she replied. It turns out that her

brother's name is Martin Hill and he's eleven years older. He and his wife, Aunt Susan, have recently begun running a hotel in a coal mining town in the Rocky Mountains. Mother says she asked Uncle Martin if they could use some help. She told him we were good at washing dishes and peeling potatoes and sweeping floors and even chopping wood. "If he would welcome us, how would you all feel about packing up and moving west?" she asked us. She was grinning! I suppose we must have looked pretty funny.

We gaped at her. Nobody spoke. We were too flabbergasted. Ten minutes before, we had not known we had an uncle. Now she was not only telling us he existed, but that he had a wife and son. What's more, she was suggesting we leave Montreal and go to live with these people we had never known existed.

We could not believe what she was saying. If this man was really our uncle, why had she kept him a secret?

She took a deep breath and began to explain. She said she could understand why we thought she must be joking, since she had never spoken to any of us about him. Our father and our uncle quarrelled years ago, and Father insisted that Uncle Martin stay out of our lives. "Sam tried to make me promise not to write to him," Mother said, and she let Father think that she stopped, but she and Uncle Martin kept in touch.

"What did they fight about?" John asked.

She did not answer right away. But finally she said that Uncle Martin sent her money when he knew we were hard up. Our father was insulted. He said we did not need charity and made Mother return the money. When Uncle Martin wrote to try to persuade him to take the help, Father sent the letter back without opening it. "It was nonsensical," Mother finished, "but your father was a stubborn man and never one to back down."

The three of us were dumbfounded by the story. Finally John, sounding unsure, asked what our uncle was like.

Mother gazed out the window and thought about her answer. Then she smiled. "When I was a child, I worshipped him," she said softly. "Our parents didn't believe in giving children sweets, but when Martin began earning, he would buy me a bag of humbugs or peppermints and slip them to me in secret."

"And he runs a hotel?" Olivia asked.

"Yes. As I said, he and Susan have just bought a hotel in a mining town in the North-West Territories. They hope to get established while the town is new. It has been a struggle, I believe, and I think they might be grateful for our help."

Mother said all this in a matter-of-fact voice, as though she had no idea how her words shocked us. I realized later that this was because she had had time to think the idea over, while we had not. We were totally stunned. We still are. Move to the North-West

Territories! It sounds like a pipe dream. To me, the Rocky Mountains are as far away as the moon.

John asked if our uncle was rich.

I think Mother counted to ten before she answered. Her lips tightened and her knuckles turned white.

Then she said he wasn't, but that there is always a lot of work to do in a hotel, especially one that has just been built a year ago.

She decided to write Uncle Martin after she learned, from Mr. Burroughs, that Father had left us in such desperate straits. Clearly, she had had no idea how Father had left things. But she did think her brother would come to our rescue.

Olivia had perked up by then. The two of us were full of questions, but she asked hers outright.

"How old is their son?" she asked.

Mother smiled at her. I think she was relieved to change the subject.

"He's about your age," she said. "His name is Mark. They just have the one boy."

I was not thinking about Mark. I was trying to imagine us moving so many miles away when John's next words hit me like a punch in the stomach.

I can't go on about it, not now. But I'll be back.

Friday, June 20, 1902

I still can't believe what John said.

"You do realize we cannot take Davy with us if we go," he declared.

I gasped. I could not believe my ears. Caring for Davy on such a long train journey would be hard, of course. But how could John think of leaving him behind?

I saw my shock mirrored on Mother's face. She stared at John as though he had turned green or grown horns.

He flushed and glared back but he did not back down. "What help could he be in a hotel? Face it, Mother. He can't do a thing, not even look after himself."

Mother's face changed. The look she gave him made me shiver. Finally she said, "I might leave *you*, John. You are sixteen and surely could find a way to support yourself. Davy, however, is utterly dependent upon us."

John began to argue. He was trying to shout her down but she kept speaking, giving him no chance to interrupt.

"Before you suggest I put your brother into an asylum, I will take you to visit one. Afterwards, when you have seen what you are talking about, we can discuss it again."

John's face grew dark. When he swung to face her, he stuttered. "But . . . but, Mother," he began, "I am sure, if Uncle Martin and Aunt Susan knew . . . "

"They *do* know," Mother snapped. "I have told them about him. I told them about all of you. We have not written frequently, but we did keep in touch."

This time, nobody spoke while she caught her breath. Then she added, "When we get an answer to my letter, we'll talk again. Now I am going to bed."

And, without another word, she went.

After a break to rest my hand

I was glad to escape to my room, where I can lie and think over everything.

Mostly I thought about Davy. He did not grow like an ordinary baby, but he did not die the way the doctor thought he might. One day, I overheard one of the ladies at church tell another that she thought his dying would have been a blessing.

When I told Mother, she said, "Consider where it comes from and ignore it."

But her eyes flashed.

Davy himself IS a blessing, even though he does need a lot of care. Not that long ago, Father said we should not have kept him because he would soon become too heavy for me to carry. He kept harping on the subject of Davy's future as though it were a sore tooth he had to keep poking

"We'll cross that bridge when we come to it," Mother would tell him. I think she cannot imagine Davy becoming a man. He gets the croup often and has almost died twice already.

We cannot go to Uncle Martin's without him. But I need not fuss because I know Mother will not let it happen, whatever John says.

Bedtime

No letter today. These days seem longer than any I have lived through before. I keep wanting to go and move the hands of the clock ahead.

I can tell that Olivia feels the same way. She plays the piano by the hour. This sometimes helps, to tell the truth. If only she did not always play such mournful pieces. Yesterday, I told her to play "Won't You Come Home Bill Bailey," and she looked at me as though I had spat on the Bible.

John is never home, or if he is, he's studying for his exams.

To make matters worse, Davy was sick today. He choked and then threw up. But we got through it.

Saturday, June 21, 1902

We had company all day. Cousins of Father's I'd never met before. I don't think I'd ever heard of them. Second cousins once removed or some such thing. Mother was polite but I could tell she did not like them any more than I did. I am sure they just came to see how things stood.

Once they were out the door, I muttered, "Nosy Parkers."

Mother looked at me. "Abby, that is rude," she said. "It is true, mind you, but it is also rude."

Her eyes were laughing so I knew she was not really angry.

Sunday, June 22, 1902

Mother has started cleaning the house with a vengeance. She has totally given up resting on the Sabbath. She is getting ready to leave. Yet this seems impossible. We have lived here as far back as I can remember. Even if this house is rented, it feels like ours.

This morning, I heard Mother laughing and went to see what the joke was. She had found a diary she wrote when she was fifteen. She let me take it away to read. It is funny, but it is also dull. There is so much about the weather and what they have for dinner. It is not at all like this notebook. I am determined not to write such dull stuff. I have nothing to say about the weather! Her sentences are too short and chopped up. Here's a typical day.

Went to school. Had stew for supper. Very cold out. Rained in afternoon. I hate helping with housework. It is never finished.

I should not say so, but I am a better writer than Mother was. Why does it matter that it rained? I agree with the bit about housework though.

Monday, June 23, 1902

Uncle Martin sent us a telegram to say we were all welcome and a letter would follow. I was the one who answered the door and there stood the boy with the telegram in his hand. I did not know what to do for a minute. I don't ever remember a telegram coming to us before. It was so good of Uncle Martin to let us know that way.

Mother read it aloud. It said: COME ONE, COME ALL. WE HAVE ROOM AND NEED HELP. LETTER FOLLOWING. LOTS OF LOVE, MARTIN.

Her eyes shone. I did not guess quite how anxious she had been until I saw how relieved she was. I hope the letter does not take a long time coming. We are full of questions.

Tuesday, June 24, 1902

Everything is at sixes and sevens. Mother is carrying on with more housecleaning. Not just dusting, but scrubbing, moving every stick of furniture, washing curtains and bedding and whatever else is in the linen closet. Even walls! I can't see why it matters. I am too tired to write about it.

Davy has to be kept out of trouble while I work on other tasks. I stop still, every so often, trying to convince myself that my world is soon going to change utterly! I can't make it feel real.

I'll write again when Uncle Martin's letter arrives.

Thursday, June 26, 1902

Mother told us today that we will be leaving on July 14. She has the tickets. And she is getting ready to sell most of our things. It is called an auction of household goods and chattels. I've never heard of a chattel before.

Friday, June 27, 1902

I am exhausted! I keep waiting for something exciting to put in here, but nothing is exciting these days. I keep wanting to cry. My hands are all rough from scrubbing with lye soap. Mother says to try using more elbow grease. I know what she means, but I don't like to be told to use it when I am doing my best already. I have broken fingernails and had to get Mother to pick out lots of splinters. Ugh!!

If Father were here, he'd make us come to sit and be lectured. I long to sit down and fold my hands in my lap and get a break from housecleaning. I don't really want to be scolded, but it would be worth it to be allowed to sit down. I would only need to whistle to bring on a scolding.

I wish I had not written that bit about Father. It is such a muddle inside me. I will be happy when this part of my life is behind me and the Western Adventure has begun. Surely we won't keep thinking about Father in a place where we have never seen him.

Sunday, June 29, 1902

The letter from Uncle Martin came in Friday's mail. It's from Frank, in the District of Alberta. It is pages long.

Uncle Martin says that Olivia can be a big help in the hotel, and Mother will be able to give a hand with the cooking. They sometimes have over twenty people for a meal, and it takes a lot of work.

It is hard to imagine cooking dinner for so many. There must be towering stacks of dishes to do. Olivia and I both gasped and, for once, when our eyes met, our thoughts were identical.

He told us that Frank is less than two years old and yet has over six hundred inhabitants, as if that were a lot. I can't remember right now how many people live here in Montreal, but it is a lot more than six hundred.

Mother says Frank is near the Crowsnest Pass, which is one of the main routes through the Rocky Mountains. That sounds exciting. I wonder if it is anything like my picture of it.

Uncle Martin said that Davy and I are welcome too. I can care for Davy and sometimes help with the other work. Then he said John will also be welcome. There is plenty for a stout lad to put his hand to. Those were his exact words.

John looked relieved but also put out. Maybe he didn't like being called a stout lad. It does sound a bit strange.

Mother folded up the letter and then told us she had checked the amount we had in the bank. There's enough to cover our expenses until we go, if we are careful. She took a deep breath and said a few of Father's friends paid back what they owed, so some of his debts are paid now. She has arranged to auction off most of our belongings to cover the rest. She thinks the dining room furniture and the piano will bring a good price.

Olivia screamed, "You cannot sell the piano. Father bought it for me. It's mine!"

I admit that the idea of selling the piano shocked me too, but Mother said Olivia must just hope there would be a piano she could play where we are going. She added that we would have to sell John's telescope too, and he was not making a fuss about that.

Olivia did not care tuppence about that telescope. To tell the truth, I don't think John treasures it himself. Father got it for him when he was twelve or so but it has never worked that well. John was excited about it when he got it, but he hasn't set it up for ages.

Olivia kept raging until John told her to be still. She glared at him but she did hush up. When he orders us around, he sounds like Father.

When she was quiet, he turned and asked Mother if she had found out what we could get for the ring.

I did not know what he meant, but Mother did.

"You know that ring is Abby's, John," she said, staring at his angry face. "What it's worth is not your concern."

I knew nothing of any ring which belonged to me. Mother looked tired enough to drop. She patted my hand.

"I will explain this to you one of these days, Abby. Now is not the time," she said.

"If it is something that we could sell," I broke in, "something you could get some money for — "

"No," Mother snapped, before John or Olivia could say a word. "Leave it be."

Then she marched out to the kitchen and started packing dishes we never use. I felt I might try raging too, but I knew it wouldn't help. I ran upstairs and slammed my bedroom door. Then Davy started to wail and I had to run back down.

I am not used to growing angry at Mother. It was horrible.

Monday, June 30, 1902

Davy is fed and now he's asleep again. But that is not what I want to write about.

After supper, when I was sorting through some old books, John came down the hall past Olivia and me and went into the parlour where Mother was writing letters. I watched and listened, hoping I would find out more about that ring or Uncle Martin's family.

Mother looked up and waited for him to join her. Then she said quietly, "You do wish to come west with us, John, or am I wrong?"

Instead of answering her, he said in a cold voice, "You told them about Davy. Do they also know about Abby?"

Mother did not answer. She just got up and closed the door with a bang. As it swung shut, I heard her say, "For pity's sake, boy, give this up."

What did John mean? Was this more about the mysterious ring? I wanted to demand an explanation, but I couldn't, not after the way she closed the door.

I slipped outside and stood by the open window, hoping to hear something more. I only caught one phrase before Olivia came after me. She grabbed my arm and pulled me back into the house without saying a word. I was furious, but I knew Mother would have hated me eavesdropping. All I caught was the phrase "no blood relation."

"You leave me be," I hissed at Olivia.

"Then don't snoop," she shot back.

I stared at her. I wanted to ask if she knew what they were talking about. But she wouldn't tell me if she did. And she doesn't. I could tell by the look in her eyes. She was as bewildered as I. I turned my back on her and went to fetch Davy. When I came back, I put him down on the carpet.

Olivia looked at him as though he were dirt under her shoe. "Do take him away, Abby," she said. "Mrs. Chambers said she might drop by after Prayer Meeting for a cup of tea with Mother. He shouldn't be here. Just look at him!"

I looked. He was drooling a little, but he cannot help that. His eyes slant a bit and they are small. I had brushed his hair earlier, but it had grown a bit tousled. I wiped his mouth off with his bib and smoothed his hair. His face is a bit flat, I guess, but what is wrong with that? He looks fine to me. But not to my sister. When she looks at him, she sees a different boy.

So I lugged him out to the kitchen and plunked him down in the tin tub for his bath. He shrieked with joy. Holding onto him is not easy, but it is fun to watch him getting so excited.

Olivia is honest, at least. She does not pretend to love him. Maybe it is because of her being with Mother when she had such a hard time bringing him into the world. But I was there too and, next to Mother, I love him better than anyone.

Tuesday, July 1, 1902

Ever since yesterday, I have been remembering the day Davy was born. His birthing took over ten hours, and he was blue and not breathing when he came out, feet first. It frightened both of us and I believe even Mrs. Nasenby, the midwife, was afraid in those first moments. She slapped the poor mite and, the minute he gulped in his first breath, she held his naked body out and told Olivia to wash him off and wrap him in a blanket while she tended to our mother.

He did not look fine then. He was slippery and a reddish blue and streaked with blood. But alive!

Olivia shrank back, shouted, "No!" and ran out of the room. So Mrs. N. pushed him into my arms instead.

He was so pitiful. His body was stiff and hard to hold. I could tell that he had to fight for every breath he drew. He was one of the homeliest babies I had ever laid eyes on, but I loved him from that first moment.

I washed him off with warm water and wrapped him in a bath towel and held him against my shoulder.

"Is he dying?" I asked her. It was hard to get the words out around the great lump in my throat but she heard me.

She shot me a look and muttered, "Let's hope so."

I clutched my new brother tighter, needing to keep him safe from all the world.

Then Olivia burst in with a pot of tea. She did not even glance at the baby. I asked if she wanted to hold him. She stared at me.

"No," she said. "He makes my skin crawl. Look at him. He's hardly human."

I could not believe she meant it. But I think she still sees him that way. And John feels much the same. They are ashamed of him, as though he can't be ours.

Mother nearly died in those first days. Mrs. Nasenby said she thought it was from losing too much blood. Olivia did everything she could to help Mother recover, everything but reach out to the baby.

I must stop. My hand is aching and so is my heart as I remember that day.

Later

From that first day, it felt, to me, as though Davy was mine. I was the person chosen to hold him and keep him safe from harm. I was supposed to be starting school, but nobody spoke of it and I stayed home.

Mother was slow to recover. Caring for him was left to me. It was not easy. I felt all thumbs. His mouth was smaller than a regular baby's and he had trouble keeping hold of a nipple and then swallowing. I had to use an eye dropper often. He cried a lot and choked in a frightening way. But even though he was so weak, Mother encouraged me, and between us we managed.

I think maybe the school sent someone to ask where I was and Mother arranged for Miss Radcliffe to teach me at home.

Did I mind not going? I have never said so, but I did. I did miss going. But I loved having lessons with Miss Radcliffe.

I must stop writing and get to sleep. Morning comes fast in the summer and there is still so much to do.

Wednesday, July 2, 1902

It is twenty days since Father was killed. Nightmare days. I lay awake most of the night thinking of the things John had let slip.

His feelings about Davy came straight from Father, who said, often, that Davy "would be better off with his own kind." He also said, "Looking after him is too much for your mother," and, "If only she would face it."

Thank goodness we won't hear this ever again once we leave. John might think it, but Mother won't let him speak the words.

I believe John and Olivia both worry that their friends will think Davy is the way he is because of something in his heredity. Mother says they are wrong.

But what did John think Mother should have told Uncle Martin about me? I wish I could ask. I also wish I knew what she meant the day Father died when she said, "I knew I could not do without you, Abby." I still don't understand it.

I was putting down my book when Davy called. He has no proper words to use, but sometimes, he almost says my name.

"Aa . . . ee," he would call. Mostly I just answer him by reaching out and stroking his cheek, but not this morning. I sat up with a jerk, gathered him into my arms and held him tight.

"Oh, Davy," I whispered into his ear. "Oh, dearest Davy! You and I are going to the far west."

My whisper tickled. He ducked his head and then he did his best to wrap his stubby arms around my neck. He was not worried by anything. He was happy. And, all at once, so was I. I knew, deep inside, that the two of us belonged together and nothing would part us.

Saturday, July 12, 1902

I have you again, dear book. You got packed in one of the boxes and I could not find you. Then Mother needed something from that box and she reached in and pulled you out. You must have been dropped in by accident. Thank fortune she discovered you.

We are leaving on Monday morning, which is unbelievable.

There's been scant time for writing in here anyway, in the last few days. We have been too busy packing and cleaning and saying goodbye and feeling lost.

Now our house is practically empty. The wagon is coming to take us and our trunks to the station. We got through watching the furniture be sold at auction. Mother was right about the piano bringing a good price. Luckily she sold it while Olivia was out with her friends.

John embarrassed me by trying to get the auctioneer to make people bid more. Finally the man told him they'd get along better without him and John went off in a huff.

Monday, July 14, 1902, on our way

The whole family are now on the train. This morning when we boarded, we reminded me of a pioneer family, except that we are in a train, not a covered wagon. We were all carrying things we wanted to have with us on the trip.

Mother had packed an enormous picnic basket and had to shove it down the aisle ahead of her with her knee. Now it is on the rack above us and I keep thinking of the devilled eggs I saw her put in. I had plenty of breakfast, but I am already longing for one of those eggs.

I thought we would never get settled in our seats. I had Davy to hold onto, of course. I got braced for him to shriek and fling himself around when we pulled out and he first saw the world outside the window moving.

It seemed to take forever. People left behind stood on the platform and waved goodbye to us. Olivia's music teacher was there and Miss Radcliffe and some of John's and Olivia's friends. When Davy began to look nervous, I hugged him tight.

"Davy boy, we're on our way west," I said into his ear, doing my best to sound full of rapture.

Davy pushed my head away and began to laugh uproariously. Maybe my whisper tickled. Anyway, it was a great relief to hear such a happy sound. You never know with Davy.

The conductor called out "All aboard!" just as they do in books. A shiver of excitement went through me. In four days, we'll reach Medicine Hat. I wonder what a Medicine Hat is. A whistle blew a long lonesome wail as the engine huffed and the whole train began to stir and rumble as though it were taking big breaths. It was coming alive.

"Frank, here we come," I announced.

An hour and a half later

I quit writing because my hand was jiggling. At last Mother is gazing up at the picnic basket with a hungry look in her eye, yet she still has not made a move to fetch it down. It is hot and stuffy in here. And it smells of soot. The windows are streaked with dirt. The seats are covered with a scratchy material and they are not very comfortable, but it is all part of the Western Adventure.

I can hear Olivia complaining. John is ordering her to hush up. I am glad that she is not sitting next to me or she'd be reading over my shoulder and I would have to stop writing what is in my heart.

I am getting lots recorded now because Davy is staring spellbound through the window and paying no attention to me. He keeps patting the glass as though to catch hold of some of the things he sees flashing by. When they vanish, he makes small sounds of astonishment. "Ooo! Ooo!"

"Yes, Davy. I do see the dog and the boy and all the other wonders," Mother just told him. "And you are being such a good boy."

He beamed at her. She and I take turns holding onto him. John and Olivia are across the aisle from us. Except for talking to Davy, we are mostly silent. I do feel like a world traveller though. Or someone in a book.

Afternoon

Mother finally gave in and we fetched down the picnic basket at last. Why does food you eat from a picnic hamper taste so much better than the dinner you eat sitting at a dining table? The shapes of things are different. The little packages are enticing. Oh, I cannot explain. But we gobbled every last bite. Even dull things like sticks of celery tasted special.

I wish I had not finished *What Katy Did*. I saw Mother pack some books but she has not produced one. When I asked her, she smiled and said, "Patience is a virtue. Get it if you can. Seldom found in woman, but never found in man."

Then she went to sleep. I realized that she must have been awake most of last night going over everything she had to do before we left, so I kept as quiet as possible.

I like gazing out the window. We pass so many houses with people coming and going. Every so often, children wave at the train and I always wave back. Davy hoots with laughter each time I do it. I can hear Olivia's breath hiss in disapproval. John just stares out their window as though we are strangers he has never met. I think we must embarrass him somehow.

"Can't you keep him quiet?" Olivia said once. She knows I can't. Anyway, why should I? He's not disturbing anybody.

Mother and I both pretended we had not heard. But Mother did get out a book and now she is reading it aloud to us. The two across the aisle are both listening although John is pretending not to.

It is by Louisa May Alcott and it is called *Little Men*. Olivia got *Little Women* last Christmas and Mother read it to us over the holidays while we sewed.

John pretended he was bored by it too, but he was never far away when she started to read.

I like this one better but Olivia won't. She wanted Jo to marry Laurie. I remember how upset she got when Jo wouldn't.

I agreed, at first, but I liked the Professor when we got to know him. It is more interesting than most romance stories. The characters seem like real people.

Olivia reminds me of Meg at times and at other times she is like Amy. I want to be like Jo. Neither of us is a bit like Beth, even though Olivia did love her piano. I do hope they have one where we are going. Everything in life goes more smoothly when my sister has a piano to keep her happy.

Later again

I had a nap while Mother held onto our "good boy." The train is crowded with other people heading west. I still haven't talked to any of them. Mother has nodded to some. Olivia has found a couple of girls her age to sit with sometimes. She has also found a boy who stares at her but says nothing. She pretends not to notice, just looks at the other girls and they all giggle. They sound mean, but maybe he likes it.

Evening

Mother pulled out a deck of cards when we were finished eating, and the others came over for a game of Hearts. Davy, bless him, had gone solidly to sleep, so we could play in peace. We are going to bed as soon as the berths are made up. I am looking forward to sleeping on the train, although sharing with Davy won't be peaceful.

Tuesday, early morning, July 15, 1902

Slept in berths last night. Olivia and Mother shared an upper one. Davy and I were underneath them. And John was across the aisle in a bed to himself. It is like having a shelf to sleep on, with a little hammock hanging down to hold things and a window with a blind to pull down and shut out the outside world. I like to watch that world go by, though.

Davy thrashed about at first. He whacked me across the nose until I hid under the pillow. He did not do it on purpose, and when I yelped, he laughed. I will have bruises. Finally he fell asleep and I lay looking out at the darkening world sliding by.

It was magical sometimes. Mysterious. At first I saw houses with lights on upstairs, and then, one by one, some of them blinked off while I watched.

Then, long after our train car was filled with sleeping passengers, I saw one house all lit up with people hurrying past bright windows. Was a baby being born? Or was a doctor rushing in to a sickbed? Or what? Maybe they were having a party. But somehow it didn't look like it. The house vanished from sight, leaving me full of curiosity. I do hope those people were celebrating.

Noon

We are crossing Ontario. We have been crossing it forever. It is enormous. And wild. Miles of dark evergreen trees and huge rocks. It is full of wilderness, lakes and forest. Today, when Mother had gone to the toilet and Olivia was in the next car chatting with her new friends, the train stopped moving. I don't know why. I looked out and saw a stag on top of a rocky hill. He was standing tall and looking so proud.

I blinked, expecting him to vanish. But he didn't. He had a huge spread of antlers and he held his head up high, as though he were wanting us to admire them.

I had to share it so I called softly to John and pointed. I expected him to ignore me, but instead he looked and he was as filled with wonder as I. He came over to kneel on the seat next to me.

"Oh, Abby," he murmured, "what a grand fellow!"

"Kingly," I said.

"Majestic," he answered as the train started to move again. We grinned at each other. It felt strange to be so at one with him.

Then, as though the stag sensed he was being watched, he raised his head, turned about and lifted into the air with one bound. He was there and then he wasn't.

The train picked up speed and then the others came clattering back. I opened my mouth to tell them, and then John and I looked at each other and neither of us said a word. As he went back to his seat, though, he grinned and winked at me.

Maybe I'll tell Mother when we are by ourselves.

Later

We still have two nights and two days to go before we get to Medicine Hat. Davy is growing used to the train whistle blowing and the rumbling wheels. He used to bounce around and try to make the same sound. It was funny to listen to him. It was also a little embarrassing. People going by would jump or laugh. Now he is calm and I actually miss his noises.

The other passengers are getting used to him, though, and they smile real smiles at him now. They have asked me what his name is.

I haven't talked to anyone my age yet. I have seen some, but I think Davy makes them feel shy.

Still later

A new boy, or maybe I should say "young man," has taken a shine to Olivia. This is always happening, of course. She is so pretty. She does not think much of him, I believe, because he is not very handsome. She is so picky. But I suppose she cannot help enjoying his worshipful eyes fixed upon her. John says he is actually going to Frank. His name is Jeremiah and he is older than she is. He wears glasses though and he is short. Olivia likes her admirers to be tall.

This one likes Davy. He called him a jim-dandy laddie. I hope Olivia heard him.

Wednesday, July 16, 1902

We have left Ontario behind finally and slept through some of Manitoba. We are really coming into the Great North West, but not quite. The train chugs along for miles and miles without us finding any of the towns named on our map. There are lakes and trees and rocks by the millions. But hardly any people. Is this what they mean when they talk of wilderness?

I got talking to the girl who moved into an empty seat behind us when Mother began reading aloud. Her name is Betsy Hunt. She is going to Regina to live with her grandmother while she attends high school. She was pretending not to listen, but now she can laugh along with the rest of us. She loves *Little Men*.

Still Wednesday

Betsy has taken the train before and she says it goes on like this forever. She's thirteen. I wish she was coming on out to Frank.

Later on

We stopped in a town I thought was Winnipeg but it wasn't. A new family with children got on. Because of staying with Davy, I don't roam up and down the train the way John and Olivia do. I wonder where they are going. There is a boy about my age and two little girls with flaming red hair. Olivia says they are snooty, but I think they are just shy. The boy's name is Connor.

Mother asked if we would like to try eating in the dining car today.

"We can't!" John muttered. "Not with Davy."

"Please, can't we go without him some time. Abby could stay with him," Olivia began.

Mother gave her an ice-cold look. Then, without saying a word, she turned her back and stared out the window. Olivia opened her mouth to say she was sorry, but shut it without speaking.

I confess that I would love to try eating in the dining car. It sounds opulent. Is that the right word? Maybe elegant is better. But Davy doesn't do well sitting at dining tables.

After what felt like hours, we stopped at a station and Mother sent John and Olivia to buy food. They got apples and stale buns. We ate without speaking. Even Davy was quiet. It was horrible. Betsy must have wondered what was wrong with us. She must wonder what is wrong with Davy but she has never asked.

Thursday, July 17, 1902

We are crossing the prairie now. It goes on for miles and miles. And then, guess what? More miles! Not wilderness exactly. Wild though. Flatter. You can see a long way and the sky is the biggest I have ever beheld. That is the right word for looking at such a grand sky. It needs a grand word.

I am glad Mother brought books. Without them, this journey would take an eternity. Canada is so HUGE!

Davy loves watching the prairie dogs popping up out of the ground and then vanishing quick as a wink.

Today a child on a horse rode up beside the train and began racing us. We were all laughing and cheering and then his hat blew off and he was a girl. How I would love to ride like that.

I worry about our fitting in when we arrive. What if they don't like us? Mother says they will, but I suspect she might be slightly worried herself. She stares out the window and sighs and wrinkles up her forehead.

It comforts me to know that they are Mother's relatives, not Father's.

We miss seeing big chunks of the country because we have to sleep. Tonight we are supposed to be in Medicine Hat. We will still have miles to go after that.

Later

I was just thinking that we hadn't seen any Indians when we stopped at a little station and there stood a whole family of them. Well, two parents and two boys. They were on the platform — meeting someone, I think. They were not one bit red-skinned but they were definitely Indians. They were talking to each other in a foreign language. Well, an Indian language.

Tonight we get to Medicine Hat. I am eager to get off this train and walk around. I feel full of twitches from sitting still. Also, Davy is getting cranky. I hope he is not getting sick.

Suppertime

The prairie we went through earlier was absolutely flat, but now the land is looking bumpier. Mother told us to start watching out for foothills. Someone on the train was pointing out ravines he called "coulees." But they aren't foothills.

We have come so far. When I tried to picture the journey before we left Montreal, it was not as unending as this. Father died just over a month ago, but I feel as though he was someone I knew in another life. It is not that I have forgotten him exactly, but our world with him in it seems unreal, not connected to where we are now. He seems no longer part of our lives, like a memory that is fading away. It troubles me a bit, but I try not to dwell on it.

I cannot believe we will get to Frank tomorrow. We have a long way to go yet, but everyone is gathering up bits and pieces and starting to look more like travellers nearing their destination.

Mother got talking to Connor's mother. They are going to Frank! We were surprised. She offered to take care of Davy while we go to the dining car. Mother said not today, but it was very kind of her to offer. Then Mother gave John some money to take Olivia there. When they had gone, she asked if I would have liked to go with them. I told her no. She said she thought I'd feel that way.

I wasn't lying exactly. I *would* like to have gone, but not without her.

After supper

The train is just sitting still. Sleeping in a berth in a train that is not moving will be strange.

The little redheads run races up and down the cars. Their names are Susie and Eileen. Eileen runs faster than Susie but S. has a friendlier grin. Every so often, Connor is sent to chase them down. He hates this. He nods to me now when he passes, but we don't speak.

When we stopped in Regina, Betsy got off. She gave me her address. She wants me to write to her.

Thursday evening

When the conductor told us we were in the District of Alberta, I stared out the window, all agog to see mountains. I had heard so much about snow-covered peaks and wild animals like elk. And what did I see? Not even a hill. There was lots of land and there were animals, but the ones I saw were cows and horses, not bears or elk or mountain lions. No eagles swooped over. It was disappointing.

I was moping over this when Connor came down the aisle and asked me what was wrong.

"No mountains," I growled.

"I promise there soon will be. Frank is built right up against one called Turtle Mountain. And there are lots higher ones," he told me.

Then he leaned down and tickled Davy on the back of the neck. Davy squealed with delight. He was not interested in snowy peaks. To him, Connor was far more exciting.

"What are your sisters up to?" I asked.

Connor laughed. "They're asleep and Mother is reading" he said. "That's why I came looking for company."

"Take my seat, Connor," Mother said. "I want to stretch, and if your mother is not too deep in her book, I'll stop for a chat with her on my way back. She makes me feel we may actually arrive."

Davy did not like her leaving, but he did like Connor staying. So did I.

"Is there really a Turtle Mountain?" I asked. Turtles seemed a bit low down to give their name to a mountain.

Connor drew me a picture. It's a sort of map. It made Frank seem like an actual town. Turtle Mountain is BIG! We kept gabbing on until Mother returned. But when Connor stood up to give her back her seat and I looked out the window, there were still no mountains in sight. There wasn't even a hill. Then we passed a belt of trees and there, on the other side, were two long-horned animals. Connor told us they were antelope. He says the buffalo are almost all gone. Davy and I were both delighted to sight real wildlife.

"Holy cow!" I said.

"Holy antelope, you mean," Connor said with a snicker.

I could not stop staring at them until we left them

behind. I have never seen wild animals roaming about freely, except for that stag. Both Davy and I have been to a circus, but that is entirely different. I felt as though I had finally caught my first glimpse of the Wild West.

"Well, that's better than staring out at nothing for hours on end," John said, looking over my shoulder.

Mother arrived back in time to hear this. She was disgusted. She says that most children never get out of their home town, and we are most of the way across an enormous country yet all we do is complain.

Connor smiled at her. "My father says Alberta is going to be made a province in the next two or three years," he told her. "Saskatchewan too."

He sounded like a Geography book. Then Davy let out a squawk. When we looked to see what he was excited about, there was an elk in the distance and more prairie dogs close to us. And, far, far away, a blur on the horizon that might even be an actual foothill.

My bad mood melted away like butter in the summer sun. I gave Mother my best smile to cheer her up and she relaxed.

Bedtime

We will have to change trains to get to Frank. There will be a lot to gather up.

John might be more helpful than he was in Montreal. He has taken Davy for a ramble two or three times, giving Mother and me a rest. It was lovely. Davy does bounce about a lot and my arms get tired sometimes. Keeping him still is impossible.

I am coming to like John better than I used to. Olivia too. We're more joined together somehow. We feel like a proper family. Most of the time anyway.

Friday, July 18, 1902, very early

We are nearly there. I feel so grubby and tired. Davy needs a bath in the worst way. He smells. He hasn't been washed properly since we left Montreal.

I would not be surprised if I smell too, although not as powerfully as Davy. Even Olivia looks crumpled, and her hair, which is usually like spun gold, looks dull and stringy.

We are excited about getting there, but also on edge. Or is that just me? I wish it were tomorrow.

I said so and Mother told me not to wish my life away. "This journey will soon be over and not only will Davy have a bath, but we'll all sleep in a proper bed," she said.

"Not all in one!" Olivia said, actually teasing her.

Mother chuckled. "Right," she said.

But I bet I share with Davy as usual.

I am packing this notebook away in my bag to keep it safe. Next time I write in it, we will be in Frank.

Friday, July 18, 1902, Frank, Alberta

We are in Frank! We are in the Four Winds Hotel as I write.

I've just fished out my notebook and will tell about our arriving while Davy naps. He is exhausted, so I might have lots of time — even though I am tired myself.

We changed trains last night and got here at dawn. "Next stop Frank," the conductor shouted, grinning at us.

Jeremiah came to help with our cases. He is so nice. He and John are good friends now. He just appears without making a fuss about it. He's like Connor.

John picked up Davy. I was surprised and so was our little brother. He whooped and smacked John on the head. I think maybe John needed somebody to hide behind when he faced unknown relatives. I understood. I was planning to use Davy that way myself.

We bumped down the aisle and then suddenly we were out on the platform, staring at a new world. The sky was such a bright blue, without a single cloud. Vivid, Miss Radcliffe would call it. There were huge looking mountains, especially one that seemed to loom over us. It scared me a little. Maybe even a lot.

Connor spoke up from right behind me. "Behold Turtle Mountain," he announced in a booming voice. Even though I felt nervous, I had to laugh. Davy bounced up and down in John's arms when he saw it. It was enormous for a turtle.

I stood staring at it, and then a breeze brushed my cheeks. It was cool and it smelled different. A tall boy who I knew must be my cousin Mark, because he looked so like Mother, was standing grinning at me. He said, "You're smelling the snow. That wind is coming from the mountains."

It felt marvellous. Like cool fingers brushing away the soot and sweat.

After a short break

Davy gave a moan and started waking up so I stopped writing, but then he went right back to sleep. It is lucky he's such a fine sleeper — lucky for my notebook.

Seeing Turtle Mountain was thrilling, but the best moment was watching this big woman, who is our aunt, wrap her arms around my mother and give her one of the most loving hugs I have ever seen. Mother hugged her back and, watching them, I felt as though this lady had lifted a great burden off Mother's shoulders. I had not seen it before, but I realized it had been there, weighing her down ever since Billy Brigson burst into our kitchen to tell us Father was dead.

The next best moment was when the same woman turned around and, ignoring me and Olivia and John, beamed at Davy and said in a voice like warm honey, "Hello, my sweet boy. May your Aunt Susan give you a welcoming kiss?"

Davy flung himself about, which made kissing him hard to do. He was dirty too, filthy from the smoke of the train smeared over his damp face. And he smelled, as I said before. But she dodged his swinging arms and gave him a smacking kiss on his nose. He hooted like a barnful of owls.

For one moment, I knew how Olivia felt when Davy was acting like a sideshow and everyone was staring. The whole world seemed to be gawking at us and I wanted to disappear.

Then I was the one being kissed and I wasn't embarrassed any longer. Olivia stepped right up for hers, but John blushed and backed away fast. He was looking around for me to rescue him from Davy.

I felt lonely seeing my baby brother being kissed by a stranger, and glad when John handed him back. Aunt Susan kept after John until he too had gotten hugged. Then Uncle Martin arrived and rescued John by holding out his hand in a manly way.

My cousin Mark had a large, gangly dog named Dulcey with him. Her droopy ears are warm and silky smooth. She has big brown eyes and a long, feathery tail, which I think she uses for smiling.

"This is Davy, Dulcey," Mark said. He patted her head and smiled up at my little brother.

Davy gave a joyful shriek, which made everyone smile. I thought he would be afraid of her, since we have never had a dog, but he adored her from the first moment.

When the train pulled out, we all waved. Uncle Martin led us to a wagon. He took the reins from the hitching post and swung up onto the driver's seat.

"Pile in," he said. "It's not far, but Susan said you'd be weary and in need of a lift. Leave the luggage. Mark will come back for it."

I rode with Davy on my lap and Mother next to me. Olivia hesitated and Aunt Susan reached out and hoisted her up to squeeze in between herself and our uncle.

Then we jolted off up the main street.

There are four hotels. All of them have been built in the past year. The whole town looks new. It is so strange after living in Montreal, which has been there for hundreds of years. Frank even smells new. And as we went along we saw that more things are being built.

"Well, Abby girl, the great adventure has begun," Mother murmured as we jostled each other. "And it is going to be wonderful. Just as I promised."

I tried to smile, but everything had come at me so all of a sudden that I could not. Then Uncle pulled the horse to a stop before a large square building, reached by wide steps. People were looking out the windows, watching us arrive.

I felt their eyes taking in our heavy winter clothes. They were crumpled and grimy and damp with sweat. I ducked my head and tripped on the bottom step. Somebody laughed and I was mortified.

Then Aunt Susan patted my back and muttered, "Keep your chin up, girl. They're curious, but friendly."

Then we were bundling through the front doors into the entrance hall of the Four Winds Hotel. We had arrived in Frank, our home to be.

Almost bedtime

We're partly settled in. Aunt Susan took me and Davy to where we'll sleep. It is on the ground floor at the far end of the staff rooms. It was a big room once but it is divided in two now. You can tell that it used to be part of the pantry. The walls have shelves going right to the ceiling. There is only space enough left over for our double bed. Next to it is a chest which holds a pitcher and basin. Inside it is the chamber pot.

It is hot and noisy there and you can smell the food cooking in the kitchen, but Davy and I have it to ourselves. If he decides to yell in the night, he won't disturb everyone.

We were given a few minutes to wash our dirty faces and hands and comb some of the tangles out of our hair.

When I had got myself and Davy cleaned up we came out to look for the others. I was amazed to find Mother and Olivia already in the kitchen lending a hand.

Aunt Susan told me that tomorrow night there would be a Sing. "In the other hotels they mostly play cards and pool. We do too, of course, but getting all the guests singing is something we really enjoy," she said.

"We will too," I told her. I had put Davy down for

a moment and I bent to pick him up again. I thought of Olivia as I straightened. "Is there a piano?" I asked. "Olivia plays wonderfully."

"A pedal organ," Aunt Susan answered.

I knew Olivia could play one of those. She knows lots of songs too, which she can play by ear. We are worn out tonight, but by tomorrow I'm pretty sure Olivia will be happy to play and sing for them.

Saturday, July 19, 1902

I had no more time for writing yesterday. I suppose I was too tired anyway. But here is what happened the rest of the day.

Poor Olivia told me that the minute she had got changed, they led her to the kitchen and gave her an apron and a paring knife. Before she had even finished tying her apron strings, a big woman called Mrs. Mutton, who turned out to be the cook, had plunked a pan of potatoes down in front of her. I had to admire my sister. She wanted to burst into tears, she said, but she got right to work without giving a peep of protest. I know she was weary and yearning to go straight to bed, but she went to work instead. Mrs. Mutton must have guessed how she was feeling.

"Welcome to life at Four Winds," she said and then she grinned and patted Olivia on her shoulder. "I am surely glad you are here, honey child. We're really short-handed tonight and no mistake — your coming is a godsend."

I heard this part. I think I am going to like Mrs. Mutton. Olivia did her best to smile, and slaved on.

Before long, a gong sounded in the hotel to say that the first seating for supper was ready.

After the Saturday-night Sing

I got Davy bathed and fed early. It was not full dark yet and there was a lot of noise, but he was tired enough that when I tucked him in, he went to sleep faster even than I hoped. Once the singing started, I planned to keep checking on him. I put a big chair up against the side of the bed in case he rolled, but he usually stays still when he first goes to sleep. I was out in the lounge by the time the crowd gathered. Aunt Susan welcomed everyone who had come. Then she said, "This is my niece, Olivia. I hear that she can play by ear. Let's give her a chance. Mrs. Dewbury can have a rest."

When I had warned Olivia this was going to happen, she had just scowled and not answered, so I held my breath. For a moment I thought she might refuse. But she does love making music, so I needn't have worried. She stepped up, took her place and rippled her hands up and down the keyboard in a grand swoosh of notes.

Then somebody called out, "Do you know the song 'Oh My Darlin' Clementine,' city miss?"

Everyone laughed, but of course she did, and next thing she had them all singing it.

I kept slipping out to check on Davy, until I found

Mother snoozing in the chair by the bed. She opened her eyes and then told me she would stay with him.

"If he wakes up, I'll be here," she said. "Go and enjoy yourself."

"Olivia is playing beautifully," I said. "And she's laughing."

Mother smiled, put her hands together, looked up at the ceiling and said, "Thank you, God."

Then I went back to the Sing. As Mark said, it was grand. Jeremiah was there, standing next to the organ. I overheard him say, "You sure can get music out of those old keys, Olivia."

It took her a second to remember her manners, but she finally broke down and gave him a smile. Bravo, Olivia!

Monday, July 21, 1902

I am liking it here. The Hills are really nice to us. I feel as though I've known them forever. But it is so different living in a hotel. I keep having to stop and think about what comes next. And even though Davy seems happy most of the time, I have to watch him every minute to keep him from disturbing people. I'm too tired and too busy to write another word tonight.

Wednesday, July 23, 1902

I know. I've missed Tuesday. But we've been occupied getting our bearings — that's what Mother calls it. But I'm here at last, pen in hand.

I took Davy outside this afternoon. I met up with Olivia as she was heading to her room. Her hair was all on end. Her face was flushed and damp with sweat and she looked as though, once she got to her room, she might never come back out. She gave a great sigh. Then she staggered off down the hallway.

I found Aunt Susan in the back garden picking lettuce. She looked tired and as though her back hurt. I put Davy down on a patch of grass and took her basket from her. She sank down on a wooden bench and sighed like Olivia.

I started picking lettuce, but had to dive to grab Davy before he got into the raspberry canes. He smiled sweetly and ate the beetle he had just caught.

I winced.

Aunt Susan laughed. "I think he enjoyed it," she said. "He's a dear child, Abby," she went on, "and he's fitting in just fine. If you are anxious about this, there's no need."

She is so nice.

Thursday, July 24, 1902

This afternoon, while Mother and Olivia helped do mountains of dishes, I took Davy outside again to look about. Never have I seen such a tall sky. It is somehow a far deeper blue than our sky in Montreal. It looks so clean and the air smells so fresh. And your eyes are drawn up to the mountaintops.

Mark went with us. Finding I have a cousin is

exciting. He's really friendly. He showed me where to look to see Crowsnest Pass. You would think it was high and narrow, a slice between towering peaks, but it is not. It goes up gradually. But it is a distance away from Frank.

Turtle Mountain looms over the valley, but it does not tower up until the crest is hidden in clouds, like Mount Everest. The only mountains I had ever seen before we came west were pictures in books. Turtle Mountain and the other mountains we can see look much more solid than those pictures.

Davy gazed up at the mountain as though it had him under a spell. It frightened me a little, but I suppose it is just because I am not used to mountains — at least, not this close. It made me feel as though I had shrunk. It shuts off the sun long before sunset, shadowing the valley.

After a minute, Mark took Davy out of my arms. "This fellow is too heavy for you to lug about everywhere," he said. "I'll take him for a while."

At home everyone, even Mother, takes it for granted that I am the one who carries Davy. I suppose it is because I started when he was tiny and I've never stopped. My arms felt empty and light as air when Mark lifted him away. I waved them up and down like wings. Thank goodness I have changed out of my serge dress. This muslin is so much cooler.

I was enjoying it when Uncle Martin appeared and called Mark to take over the telegraph for a while. I didn't know what he meant, but I followed along as he headed for the boxcar which they are using for a station until they build a permanent one. Mark said to come and see him operate the telegraph. Inside the boxcar was a pot-bellied stove with seats where I could sit with Davy on my lap. Mark explained that telegraph messages keep arriving, and when my uncle has to do something else, Mark takes over sending and receiving them. He was proud of doing this and I didn't blame him.

He set Davy on the floor and sat down at the machine. It is big and complicated looking. As I watched him getting set to work, I found myself longing to try it. I don't know what gave me the courage, but when he finished tapping out a message to be sent, I actually astonished myself by asking Mark if he would teach me the Morse Code.

"Surely," he said, as though I had asked him to pass the butter.

I wanted to know if he thought a girl could do what he was doing, but before I ask, I should learn the code. I might get so quick at it that I will impress him. I think I'll have to surprise more than just Mark. It looks difficult. But I like puzzles.

I like Mark and Uncle Martin too. He is more easygoing than Father was. He laughs a lot. Father hardly ever laughed. But that does not mean Uncle Martin thinks girls are equal to boys. I think hardly any adults believe that, although Mother does. I asked her once and she said, "Of course." She sounded surprised at my having to ask such a question.

While we were talking, the telegraph began to click and clack and Mark took the message and sent an answer.

I will watch him every chance I get. I'm almost sure I could do it. Keeping an eye on Davy is the only problem. You can't let your mind wander. He has begun to crawl. He moves like a clumsy lightning bug and can escape if you forget him.

Friday, August 1, 1902, early

I want to write in here when interesting things happen. But now that we are in Frank, I am too busy. The days are so full of hotel guests needing things and my having to tend Davy and trying to find time to watch Mark or Uncle Martin so I can learn Morse Code in secret. I also help in the kitchen sometimes when Davy's asleep.

After supper

This morning, while I was waiting for the train to come in, I worked on the Morse Code. I say it out loud and Davy laughs. He tries to copy the sounds I make. He is so funny.

"Da . . . da . . . do . . . dumda . . . dodee . . . daaa."

—◊—

Saturday, August 2, 1902

Olivia is so strange. I know working in the kitchen makes her feel tired and fretful a lot of the time. But this morning I offered to take over and let her sit down on the bench outside and rest for a bit. All she would have had to do was watch Davy playing on the grass.

She looked at me as though I had suggested she dance naked at dinner. Then she turned her back and walked off without a word.

I cannot understand her. I was trying to give her a break from working in the kitchen. I would far rather care for Davy than slave in there. It is not only hot, but incredibly noisy.

Mrs. Mutton also yells a lot. She has a temper the like of which I have never heard. Mother has warned us against copying her language. I would never use most of her expressions — although once in a while, she comes out with such a humdinger, I have to store it away to use in private.

Yesterday I sat down on the stairs for a moment's rest with Davy on my knee. Mrs. Mutton saw us from the upstairs landing. She laughed and called down, "You can never tell, from where you sit, where the man in the gallery's going to spit." Then she positively whooped with laughter. And Davy and I joined in. Laughter is as catching as yawning.

Tomorrow a crowd is coming, sightseers on their way through the Rockies. If only they did not all need to eat so heartily during their rest stop! The stacks of dishes tower up like mountain peaks.

Yesterday, though, a woman stopped to smile at me and give Davy a pat on the cheek. "Take good care of him, dearie," she said softly. "He's one of God's angels come down to visit."

Davy had just kicked me in the shin, so I was not so sure about his being an angel. But it was nice of her.

Tuesday, August 5, 1902

I had a lesson in bread-making today from Mrs. Mutton. Davy kept pulling at my leg to make me stop, but she swept him up in her arms and went on teaching me. The loaves are in the oven as I write. I'll take Davy out to look at his mountain while I wait. Oh, I do hope the bread does not come out heavy as lead.

I have got the Morse Code down pat and I am getting up my courage to try to send out a telegram with Mark's help.

There is a bite to the wind now. It has never been really hot though because of the mountain breezes. Mark says snow will come by Thanksgiving, but I doubt it. I wonder if Davy remembers snow.

Sunday, August 10, 1902

I did it. I proved to Mark that I knew the Morse Code forwards and backwards. So today he let me receive a telegraphed message. It was a dull one.

BE THERE AT SEVEN STOP TWO ADULTS

PLUS CHILD STOP NEED ONE NIGHTS LODGING STOP REGINALD CHART

Still, it was the most exciting thing I have ever done. Little did Mr. Chart know who was taking down his words. Clickety . . . clack. Dot . . . dot . . . dash.

Later a crowd arrived and asked for someone to guide them up through Crowsnest Pass. I wanted to go, but couldn't. Mark says that one of these days he will arrange a trip that I can join. People go through it to get to the coast.

Monday, August 11, 1902

Davy and I spotted two eagles today. He hooted and whooped but I think he was scared when one spread its wings out wide and came coasting down to snatch up a rabbit. Or was I the one who was frightened?

I admit it. I think my heart stopped for a full minute. And my eyes stretched wide. Those eagles were as grand as the stag John and I saw from the train.

And the poor rabbit did not have time to think.

Thursday, August 14, 1902

Uncle Martin found out about my learning to send and record telegrams and he was pleased as punch. There is so much work to do here and now I can be more help. Davy comes along, of course, and plays at my feet. He has a homemade toy truck now. He adores it. He runs it back and forth and makes engine noises.

The air in the mountains is thinner than the air in Montreal so Davy gets out of breath more, but it does not seem to bother him. Doctor Malcolmson was at the hotel when Davy choked on a prune pit and he turned him upside down and made him cough it up quick as a wink. He says Davy's shortness of breath is partly the altitude and partly because he has a damaged heart. This is often the way with such children. We were relieved when he told us it was nothing we need worry about.

Davy holds onto the ledge of the small window in our room and gazes out at the mountains with fascination. I wish he could tell me what he is thinking or maybe feeling. His eyes shine so.

"It's called Turtle Mountain," I told him. And I showed him a turtle in a book in the lounge bookshelf. He looked, but he did not know why he was looking. I'll have to watch out for a real turtle so he can see it and maybe understand.

Friday, August 15, 1902

Today a new family arrived. They are staying overnight. There is a woman with three rowdy boys. When I came out onto the verandah with Davy, the biggest pulled up the corners of his eyes and called out, "Look at the retarded boy."

Davy didn't know what the boy meant, but I wanted to punch him. His mother actually laughed. "Ronnie's such a card," she said. "I can't do a thing with him. But I guess boys will be boys."

Everyone was there but none of us laughed. Even Olivia gave the woman a withering stare. But Mother astonished us. She smiled sweetly at the woman and said, "Perhaps his father will teach him some manners as he grows older."

The woman flounced away and Aunt Susan clapped her hands. "Well said, Eleanor!" she remarked, loudly enough for everybody to hear.

I hope Davy never understands such nastiness.

After supper

I took Davy out for a walk today. I was carrying him when I stepped on a loose stone and fell flat. I did manage to hold him up, so he did not get hurt, but I could do nothing to save myself. I landed hard on my elbow and I felt my poor ankle sort of rip. It hurt so much that I could not get up.

When I let go of him, Davy crawled away. I tried to go after him but I couldn't. He was frightened when he saw me start to cry and he would not come to me. I didn't know what to do. We were out of sight of the hotel, hidden behind a clump of trees.

Then an Indian girl and her mother rode up on a pony. The mother — whose name is Mrs. Fairchild — went on to the hotel to get help and the girl — Nellie — stayed with me.

She was so kind. She did not say anything at first, but Davy crawled over to her and put his head down on her lap and this made us both laugh.

While we waited for her mother to bring help, the girl told me her true name means Bluebird. She said that the minister said it sounded heathen and changed it to Nellie.

I think Bluebird is beautiful, far nicer than Nellie. I said I would call her Bird and she nodded. Then her mother came back with Mark to help and they lifted me onto their pony and led her back to the hotel. Mark brought Davy.

Mrs. Fairchild has come to work at the hotel so she and Bird are staying in one of the staff rooms not far from me and Davy, which is nice.

I ended up with what Aunt Susan says is a humdinger of a sprain. She thought at first that I might have broken it, but Dr. Malcolmson stopped by and after wiggling it back and forth, he said it was not a break. He bandaged it tightly and I am supposed to keep it propped up on a chair. Mother gave me a little laudanum, but it still throbs. It is going to be awkward too, trying to mind Davy with a sprained ankle.

Saturday, August 16, 1902

Davy was staring out the window at Turtle Mountain again and Bird saw him. When I told her how he loves looking at it, she said he must *never* go there. She told me that her people call it "the mountain that walks." She couldn't explain why, but she was deadly serious.

I was talking to Mark later on and I told him what Bird had said. He just laughed. He said no mountain that size could go very far, however hard it rumbled. He says the rumbling comes from inside it.

When I looked scared, he thought it was funny. I suppose he is used to it, but I think it sounds frightening. Ominous — that's the perfect word.

"The Indians are very superstitious," Mark finished up.

I did not like the tone in his voice when he said this. It sounded as though he thought Bluebird and her people are not as smart as we are. He went on to tell me about a place called Head-Smashed-In Buffalo Jump. I think that was it. Buffalo used to go over a cliff there or something. Maybe they were driven over the cliff by hunters. I think it would be terrible to live in a town with such a name. It certainly sounds violent and cruel as well as a bit comical.

Sunday morning, August 17, 1902

The family went to church without me. Bird is keeping track of Davy since I am supposed to sit still and keep my foot propped up. It is tedious. Thank goodness I have a good book to read. When I don't have a book, I feel lonely.

Monday, August 18, 1902

My ankle feels a lot better today.

I had to take a sad telegram message this morning.

It was hard to deliver. It was to tell one of the guests that his mother had died. I hobbled around trying to find Mark or Uncle Martin to take it in to the man, but I couldn't. So I had to go myself. The man had tears in his eyes when he thanked me, and he asked me to send an answer back for him. I was proud I knew how.

I limp along trying to hold Davy with one arm and the cane Uncle Martin loaned me with my free hand. We are quite a sight.

Bird was serious about staying away from the mountain. Her eyes grow wide when it is mentioned. When she hears anyone talking about opening a new section of the mine, she almost begins to tremble. Her grandfather says danger is waiting. Danger and even death. She believes her grandfather is the wisest man in the world.

Whenever the mountain is mentioned, he shakes his head and grows upset. I'll bet he has heard about the way it rumbles and loose pieces of coal fall down inside. It frightens me to think about this.

Tuesday, August 19, 1902

I helped with canning all day. My ankle is throbbing now and I'm too tired to write.

Wednesday, August 20, 1902

Uncle Martin and Aunt Susan have told Mother I must go to school! Uncle Martin said I was far too intelligent to do nothing but mind Davy. He also said

I had showed how quickly I learned things by mastering the Morse Code so speedily. Mother wants me to go too, of course, but she is worried about Davy. Aunt Susan said firmly that there are plenty of people here to keep an eye on him.

"Olivia for one," she said. "He is her brother too and it is time she faced that fact. She should grow to know him. She hardly looks at the child, let alone helping out with his care."

I was sitting silent in the corner, not believing my ears, but when she brought up Olivia, I had to speak.

"Davy is afraid of her," I told them.

"Abby, stop talking to the floor. We can't make out what you're saying. What was that?" Uncle Martin boomed at me.

"Davy is afraid of Olivia," I said, looking straight at them. "She is ashamed of him and somehow, he knows. When he sees her coming near, he crawls away."

"If she cannot help, someone else can. Maybe Nellie could be hired to do it. They could use the money and she seems to like him. I have seen her smiling at him, and that girl is not given to smiling," Aunt Susan said.

"But she'll be going to school herself, won't she?" I asked.

"No, their family lives near Pincher Creek," Uncle Martin said. "But when her mother is working here, she often brings the girl with her. Mrs. Fairchild might not mind staying here into the fall and keeping Nellie out for a while."

"We'll discuss it with them later," Aunt Susan said. "We'll see what the new teacher thinks too. She's arriving this afternoon and she's going to be living here at first. I'm sure we can work it out somehow. But you must go, Abby. We believe in education here." She sounded as though she was serious — stuffy almost — not as jolly as she usually sounds.

I wonder what will happen. I love the thought of going to school! And Davy does like Bird. But keeping him out of trouble is not always so easy.

Later

The new teacher has come. She is young and pretty, which surprised me. Uncle Martin says she will have trouble with the big boys, but Aunt Susan claims she will have them eating out of her hand in no time. Her name is Jemima Wellington.

Mother likes her. She took her on a tour of the hotel. When they came back down, I heard Miss Wellington say, "Thank you for filling me in. It helps to know a child's background."

I wonder which child Mother was telling her about.

Friday, August 22, 1902

Miss Wellington made friends with Davy and me today. Can you say that about a teacher? Yes, I think you can. She came outside where we were rolling a ball back and forth and she sat and watched. Then she reached out and caught the ball and rolled it to Davy. He saw it coming from a new direction and just sat until it rolled against his leg. Then he made one of his chortles and rolled it away, not to her or to me but between us. We both went after it and Davy laughed as we bumped heads. Then he lay down on the ground and closed his eyes, which means "Stop, Abby."

Miss Wellington turned to smile at me. Her smile lights up her whole face. Then she asked me how I would feel about his coming to school with me for a bit. He would be able to see me, but he would get used to someone else taking care of him. If I liked the notion, she would ask Bird's mother if Bird could mind him.

I felt myself grinning and I said it would be great.

Saturday, August 23, 1902

Aunt Susan went to Bird's mother and asked if "Nellie" would like the job of helping with Davy in the schoolroom. They will pay her. Her mother thought it would be fine and Bird did, too, of course. As usual, she looked serious when the grown-ups could see, and when they went away, she grinned. She looks like two different girls.

So Bird and I are going to school together after all. If Davy is good, maybe she can stay longer. She likes reading too. Her father taught her, she says. He has been away working in the city somewhere, but he does sound nice. She has a copy of *Pilgrim's Progress* he gave her. He got it second-hand. It says in the front, *For Flossie, with her Mama's dearest love.* Bird and I wish we knew who Flossie was.

I tried to read this book when we lived in Montreal, but it was not easy. I liked some parts, but not all. The March girls in *Little Women* have copies and act it out but I did not like it as much as they did. Maybe they had fewer storybooks then.

Later

Bird's father has come home for a few days. He came to the hotel this afternoon and took them to visit some relatives who live nearer Pincher Creek and he has also forbidden Bird to go near Turtle Mountain. He agrees with her grandfather that it is perilous. That is the word he uses. She shivers when the subject comes up. I don't like it either.

Sunday, August 24, 1902

Mark says he can smell snow but I think he's teasing me. I thought it would not snow before November.

Davy is going to be thrilled. He loves watching things that move — blowing leaves or racing squirrels or flying birds. He might remember snow. But I think snow here will be different from Montreal snow.

Wednesday, August 27, 1902

I keep skipping days in this notebook, but life is so busy right now. We have all the regular work, and we are getting me set to start school. Mother is making me a skirt and a sailor blouse.

I met Jeremiah's younger sister today. She is a darling little girl. Her name is Polly. She likes walking with Jeremiah and holding hands. She has straight black hair that hangs down over her eyebrows, and huge brown eyes. Most of the time she looks very solemn and then, all at once, she beams at you and it is like the sun shining through a chink in the clouds.

I keep thinking about school. It will start soon.

Saturday, August 30, 1902

Davy took his first step alone! He was standing holding onto a chair as usual and then, all at once, he let go of the chair, took one step and sat down with a flump on his bottom. He was not hurt at all, but he surprised himself and astounded me.

When I stood him up and put his hands back on the chair, he stared at the carpet as though he was puzzling it out. Once I was back sitting down, he did it again, very carefully and slowly.

Bump!

They say people's mouths drop open in surprise. I am sure mine did. My little brother got up slowly and stood still for a moment. Then he did it for the third time and laughed. Maybe by the time he goes to school with us next Tuesday he will be taking more than one step at a time. He doesn't hurt himself. His thick nappies soften his landing, but that is not the whole story. Having such short, stubby legs is part of it. He hasn't far to fall and he doesn't topple exactly. He sinks.

He was so proud of himself. When I called them, everyone — even Olivia — came to applaud.

Sunday, August 31, 1902

Davy and Bird and I went with Miss Wellington to the schoolhouse today. We swept the floor and cleaned the blackboard and took the erasers out and banged them on the outside wall. Davy loved helping with that part, although he dropped the erasers often and got covered with chalk dust.

Miss Wellington had boxes of books and pictures to sort out. She had brought them from her home. She had other supplies too. It was exciting smelling the chalk and crayons and mixing up paints and making paste.

Labour Day
Monday, September 1, 1902

Today is my twelfth birthday. That's why I am up so early. Are they remembering? Surely Mother will. But everything is so different here and everyone is so busy. She hasn't mentioned it.

After breakfast, we are going back to the school

with more things for Miss Wellington's classroom. My ankle still twinges, which will give me an excuse to sit down sometimes.

I had just written that much when Mother slipped into my room and quietly wished me a happy day. She kissed me then and gave me a mechanical pencil to use when I write in my notebook. It is great! You don't have to worry about upsetting the ink bottle or making blots.

We did not mention my birthday at breakfast. I told Mother I thought she had forgotten; she looked at me as though I was a stranger. Then she said, "Never would I forget my Abby."

I asked her what time of day I was born, but she did not answer. When I asked again, she said she couldn't remember. I can hardly believe this, but she left the room before I could press her.

Olivia said she was born at three in the afternoon. She sounded so smug that I changed the subject.

Afternoon

Mark has been hanging up pictures and maps for our class.

I am getting excited about coming here tomorrow as a proper pupil. Bird is too, although she is not letting it show. I think she's afraid something will go wrong and she won't be allowed to come after all.

I wish Davy could understand what will happen. He liked being there with us doing the cleaning and sorting. He unsorted things, but nobody minded.

While we stopped to eat our lunch sandwiches, I let out the news that it is my birthday. Everyone clapped and sang. It was lovely.

Then Miss Wellington made us come home early and she slipped out to the kitchen to speak to Mrs. Mutton. I should have guessed, but I didn't. Luckily we had supper a bit late and, at the finish, in they came with an iced cake and candles and wished me a happy birthday.

Mrs. Mutton told me I should have said something earlier on and she could have made me a special cake. This was one she had ready for dessert, but when Miss Wellington told her what day it was, she made special icing and put in the candles.

I told her it was the proudest birthday cake I had ever had. I didn't say that I did not have one at all before we moved to Alberta. Father did not believe in celebrating birthdays. "Gimmie, gimmie days," he called them. Mother would quietly wish us a happy time, but Father acted as though it was the same as any other day.

Yet when I went to bed, there were two parcels on my pillow. One was from Aunt Susan. It is a beautiful blue scarf which she says matches my eyes. The other is a book of poems. It isn't new. In the front *Jemima Wellington* is written in black ink. Miss W. has written in *From* over her name and then *for Abby* in blue ink underneath. Then it says *Happy Birthday for a girl who loves poems*. She must have heard me reciting the

Robert Louis Stevenson poem about swinging when I was pushing Davy yesterday.

Anyway, I am now TWELVE! And I had a cake and presents! Davy is asleep so I can read poems before I put out the lamp.

Tuesday, September 2, 1902
First day of school

We started attending officially this morning.

Miss Wellington was already there when we clustered outside the classroom door. She smiled and said good morning to each of us as we arrived. I had Davy by the hand, but when he saw Bird waiting inside, he tried to trundle over to her. He managed a step before he had to crawl. I was glad and sad at the same time.

When the clock struck nine, Miss Wellington lined us up and took something from her pocket. We were astonished when she began to play a song on a mouth organ and we found ourselves marching into our classroom. She played "God Save the King" too. I still feel strange singing "king" instead of "queen." Then we said The Lord's Prayer and took our seats. I was going to school at last. It was hard to believe.

Bird and Davy have a table right behind my desk and Miss Wellington had put things there for them to do. There was a jar of big buttons to string on a shoelace. He loves doing it. When they are all strung, he takes them off carefully and starts all over. And Bird murmurs, "Good, Davy."

Davy loved that. I wanted to hug her but I couldn't, not at school.

Connor was there. So was Jeremiah's cousin Mary Ruth and some other girls my age. Two of them are named Priscilla and Mildred. They looked sideways at Davy and poked each other. Jeremiah's little sister Polly is the youngest in the class. Connor's sisters are too young to come to school yet. But Connor sat right across the aisle from me. There is another small boy called Joseph who is extremely shy. He kept his head down and never spoke a word.

It was nice to see some familiar faces.

Davy, with Bird holding onto him, stood at the window gazing out, watching leaves fall from the schoolyard trees, as wide-eyed as he can get, softly making "oooh" sounds. He certainly was no trouble. Bird stayed right with him, looking serious and not meeting anyone's eyes but mine.

After a bit, Miss Wellington quietly took her a book to read. It was *Alice's Adventures in Wonderland*. Bird's face brightened. She moved so Davy was still steady and began to read *Alice*. We were all three of us totally happy.

When it was time for recess, Bird stayed with Davy but the teacher told me to go out and breathe some fresh air.

I'll tell what happened then, later.

———

After supper

At recess, Mildred and Priscilla came up and began asking about Davy. They pretended they were interested, but really they were being mean. I tried to keep my face blank, but it was hard.

"What's wrong with your brother?" Priscilla said in a sugary voice. "Why do his eyes slant like that?"

She was smiling but it was a put-on smile, not friendly.

I didn't know what to say so I did not say anything.

"He must be foreign," Mildred said. She smirked and gave Priscilla a jab with her elbow.

"Stop it, you two," Mary Ruth told them.

I remembered she was Jeremiah's cousin and I felt grateful, even though she did not smile at me. When I saw her in school today, I thought back to when we arrived in Frank. She was at the station to meet Jeremiah. She looked me over with eyes filled with questions, but she did not speak.

Jeremiah said, "Greetings, Mary Ruth. Why don't you try saying 'Hello'?" in a loud voice. But she went red and stepped aside with a swish of her long skirt. I wish he hadn't teased her. She seems nicer than Mildred and Priscilla.

"Are those noises he makes meant to be words?" Priscilla asked, as though Mary Ruth had not spoken.

I longed to slap her face. I told them to watch what they were saying or I would report them to Miss Wellington.

"Teacher's pet," Mildred jeered.

"Quit that," Mary Ruth snapped.

Priscilla sniffed and backed away.

Mildred tossed her head and announced that her mother would not like her being at school with a red Indian and a backward boy.

None of us had seen Miss Wellington come out. She stood silently listening. She did not speak until Mildred finished. Then she said in an ice-cold voice that she would go over to have a talk with Mildred's mother as soon as school was dismissed.

"If they want me to stay and teach here," she said quietly, "Davy and Bird will stay too."

I knew from something Uncle Martin had said that getting a teacher to come to Frank had not been easy. I longed to cheer. Mildred went very red and said please don't talk to her mother. She had not meant anything rude. She was sorry.

Mary Ruth moved so her back was turned toward Miss Wellington. Then she winked at me and grinned. I think I will get to like her even if she is a bit pushy. I think she enjoys being the boss. I wanted to wink back but I couldn't. Miss Wellington would have caught me.

We all went back in and no more was said. I saw another teacher talking to Miss Wellington later, looking worried, but Miss Wellington just laughed.

Mother is giving Davy a bath, so I can keep on writing.

When school was over, Mark was waiting in front with the wagon to give us a ride home on our first day. It is a long way to lug Davy.

"We've got room for you, Mildred," he called. She lives behind the hotel.

It is plain to see that she is sweet on Mark. (She's not the only one.) She was a bit flushed, but she climbed in. Davy patted her arm. She was wearing a bracelet. "Ooooh!" he said, smiling at her. She started to snatch her arm away, but then she stopped herself and smiled back. It was a weak smile — but still, a smile.

I had schoolwork to do tonight. I have forgotten a lot. I had to review my times tables, for one thing, and study a list of Spelling words. Davy went to sleep early, which was a blessing.

When I was putting on my nightgown, Mother told me the teacher had said it was no trouble having Davy there with me today. I don't think she told Mother about Pris and Mildred. I'm relieved. It would make Mother sad. And angry.

I just had a surprising thought. Could it be that Mildred is jealous of the extra attention Davy and I are getting and that's what made her call me "teacher's pet". Miss Wellington is being awfully nice to us. I think she really likes Davy.

I did hear one other bit Miss Wellington said, which pleased me. "I believe it will make Abby's life easier if she has her brother nearby," she told Mother and Aunt Susan after supper. "Otherwise, she would be worrying about how he was getting along without her. She's a fine sister, is Abby."

I do try. It was nice to have someone notice.

Wednesday, September 10, 1902

Things are better at school now. What with homework, looking after Davy and helping to send and receive telegrams, I don't have as much time to write in this journal though. Well, I am also reading more. Miss Wellington had some books sent out from her home and most of them I have not read. I am reading *Black Beauty* at the moment. It is wonderful, although it is heartbreaking at times. There are tear stains on some of the saddest pages.

I believe they are Miss Wellington's and they are always on pages that have brought tears to my eyes too.

I planned not to write about the weather in Frank, but the wind here is not something you can ignore. Frank doesn't have breezes. It has gales. You have to hold onto your hat at all times or you would lose it for sure. It also blows your skirt up, which is embarrassing. If I don't have Davy in my arms and it is not too cold, it feels exciting sometimes. When I do have him, though, I'm afraid it may knock us flat. He isn't afraid. He shrieks with glee when it slams into us.

Four Winds is a perfect name for a hotel in this town.

Friday, September 12, 1902

Bird is reading the *Alice* book now. She's at the part where the playing cards come to life. Her mother won't have any playing cards at their place. Bird says it has something to do with her father, but she is not sure what. We have lots at the hotel. When people stay overnight, they often play cards all evening. Olivia has learned to play pool and several card games. "A veritable card shark," Uncle Martin called her. Mother is not sure it is something a young lady should do, but Olivia thinks she is just being old-fashioned. Uncle Martin stands up for my sister. I think the guests like it when she plays because she is not just pretty but she has such fun. She never showed this side of herself in Montreal.

Jeremiah likes playing games too. He and John are great friends even though John is so much younger, but I think, in his heart of hearts, it is Olivia that Jeremiah comes to see. I have watched his eyes follow her wherever she goes. I just wish Olivia appreciated him, but she is bowled over by a boy from outside Frank. He's named Tony Minelli. He is too old for her and he's incredibly conceited. Whenever nobody is watching, he poses in front of the hall mirror and combs his hair. Then he gives his head a little toss and smirks. It's disgusting.

Olivia does not speak of him if Mother is nearby. She pretends to be busy with small chores, putting away napkins or straightening out the cutlery drawer. When Mother is not looking, though, Olivia slips out the back door and doesn't come back for ages.

Mary Ruth told me that she has seen Tony taking other girls out when Olivia is doing dishes or hanging out laundry. She saw him kissing Mabel once.

I told John that and asked if I ought to tell Mother. But he just said to mind my own business. Yet I don't think he knows Tony all that well. If he did, he might change his tune. I don't like tattletales, but sometimes it is important that people know the truth.

Sunday, September 14, 1902

I went to church with Aunt Susan this morning. The singing was grand. It practically lifted the roof off. And I get a break from Davy. I shouldn't say so, but I do need to escape once in a while. It is a relief just to be me instead of always the big sister.

Saturday, September 20, 1902

I've been too busy with school to keep you caught up. Also I wrote Miss Radcliffe a long letter. It took me three days to finish. She says she likes to know all the details of our life here.

I taught Bird to play Gin Rummy today. She feels guilty when she plays cards, but she does like playing and we don't play for money, not even pennies.

Sunday, September 21, 1902

John told me today that he is getting a job in the mine. He has not liked doing fetch and carry kind of work at Four Winds. The guests order him around as though he isn't a person or even a servant, so I don't blame him for wanting to get away. But I wish he was not planning to try working in the mine. He's only sixteen, but some of the miners are as young as that. The very idea scares me. I tried to talk him out of it, but he told me again to mind my own affairs. He can be maddening.

It is strange, but I can't help worrying about him and Olivia, even though they don't care about me much. He has started drinking. He does it because that's what the men do. Not Jeremiah though.

I have heard Aunt Susan telling John what alcohol can do to a boy, but although he is polite to her, he goes right ahead when she isn't paying attention. "It's my life," he mutters under his breath.

But yesterday there was a moment that made me forgive him. That woman with the obnoxious boys is staying here again and the really nasty one began to tease Davy.

He reached out when Davy was taking a teetering step and pushed him over on purpose. It was a real shove and Davy landed heavily and whacked his head on the floor.

I saw the whole thing happen and I wanted to smack the boy, but I couldn't hit one of the guests. I picked Davy up and comforted him. He had never been treated so roughly and he was in tears.

Then all at once, in the middle of laughing loudly,

the boy let out a yell, clapped his hand to his bottom and glared at John. "You kicked me!" he shouted.

John swung around and put on a so-sorry look. "I don't believe I could have done such a thing," he said. "It wouldn't have been fair, not when you're so much smaller than I am."

I couldn't help grinning. The rotten boy is over twice as big as Davy! Then John winked at me. And Davy, seeing me grin, laughed. It was perfect.

Monday, September 22, 1902

Tonight Uncle Martin said a strange thing to Aunt Susan. Mother had just called me to bring Davy to her to have his fingernails cut. I was halfway there when Uncle Martin glanced down over the banister and smiled at us. Then he went into the room where Aunt Susan was sorting out the clean laundry and I heard him say, "The day my father rescued that child was surely a lucky day for Eleanor."

"Keep your voice down, Martin, for mercy's sake," Aunt Susan said.

Then one of them closed the door opening into the upstairs hall, and I could not hear their words any longer. I had gone up a few steps to try to listen, when Mother stuck her head out of her room and spotted us.

"Are you coming here so I can trim your brother's nails or have you and he taken root out there?" she asked.

"We're coming," I said. I felt as though she had caught me eavesdropping. Well, she had.

Once I reached her, I wanted to ask what Uncle Martin meant about his father rescuing someone. But I didn't. I don't know why. I suppose it was because of the way Aunt Susan had closed the door and hushed him.

I watched Mother cutting Davy's nails, and I pushed Uncle Martin's words out of my mind until now that I'm by myself. It is still mysterious. Aunt Susan acted as if there were a secret they were supposed to keep. Secrets seem to pile up around me.

Saturday, September 27, 1902

I know, I skipped a few days. I am so busy right now. There are heaps of schoolwork. I write to Miss Radcliffe too. I help more in the kitchen now. I am becoming a good bread maker. Then there is *Black Beauty* waiting for me. Miss Wellington has another one I really want to read too. It's called *Nobody's Boy*. I don't know why I like sad books so much, sad books with happy endings.

Thursday, October 2, 1902

Autumn is here. It even feels like winter. The snow stays on the ground most of the time and the mountains are crowned with it, even the lower ones. The wind cuts into you like a butcher knife. It makes my face ache.

Davy likes playing in the snow until he gets too cold and wet. Then he starts to wail. This happens in no time flat. It is infuriating to get him into warm clothes and take him out and then, in about five minutes, he puts his arms up to be taken back in.

He is walking a little better every day. He totters two or three steps and then down he plunks. But he never hurts himself and he gets up and staggers on again. He's saying more, but it is still hard to understand him.

I do wish Olivia would help me with him sometimes. I love him but he is a nuisance all the same. Now he is walking a bit, it is much harder. You can't count on his staying where you left him. And he is growing heavy. Father said he would.

Tuesday, October 7, 1902

Somebody mentioned Christmas today. It gives me a funny feeling thinking of spending Christmas here in Frank. It is less than three months away, though.

Mrs. Mutton is starting to plan her Christmas baking. She told me that she makes certain things every year, but always makes one dish she has never tried before. She has not yet decided what it will be this time. Last year, she made a fancy kind of braided bread.

Thursday, October 9, 1902

At school today I spelled down the whole class in our spelling bee. Bird says I should have seen the look on Priscilla's face. She has been the champion up to now. Bird heard the others talking about it. Mary Ruth was not thrilled either. But she does not like Priscilla much, so she did not mind her losing out.

Do I sound smug? It is because I am!

Tonight I was reading my poetry book and I found a funny little poem I loved. I read it out loud to Mother. It is by Emily Dickinson and it goes something like this.

> *I'm Nobody. Who are you?*
> *Are you – Nobody – too?*
> *How dreadful – to be – Somebody*
> *How public – like a Frog –*
> *Telling his name – the livelong June –*
> *To an admiring Bog.*

When I finished reciting it, John burst out laughing. "That's pretty funny, coming from you, Abby," he said. Then he went banging out the door.

"What does he mean?" I asked Mother.

She shot an angry look after John and shook her head. I waited for her to answer my question but she didn't. "The part about the frog is lovely," she said instead. "Emily Dickinson always says so much in so few words. Do you know the one that starts, 'I never saw a Moor . . . '?"

I didn't so she recited it to me. Then I told her how Miss Wellington had asked Olivia to play the organ at the Christmas concert and she said she would. Mother was pleased as punch. "She's starting to belong here," she murmured. I guess she is, but I still wonder what John meant. I was going to ask Mother again, but she got up and left the room, so I had to let it go.

Friday, October 10, 1902

Davy is more independent now. He does not need me for everything. For instance, he can take off his socks without any help. He can feed himself bread and butter too, although he smears the butter all over his funny face.

Harvest Home, October 12, 1902

Mrs. Mutton has made pumpkin pies. Thirteen of them! Pumpkin is my very favourite pie. The other thing I love is not the turkey but the dressing that goes inside it. Yummm!

Monday, October 13, 1902

Hallowe'en will be coming up before too long. I wonder if they do the same things here that we did in Montreal. Davy might be old enough to enjoy it more if they have jack-o'-lanterns and candy. Back in Montreal we ducked for apples too. He was in bed and didn't know about it. We couldn't make a big celebration out of it because of Father not liking that kind of thing. He didn't mind our *making* fudge and taffy one bit, though. Mother said he had a sweet tooth, and that was certainly true.

Friday, October 17, 1902

There's a lot of studying to do at school these days. I don't have anything much I want to write about. Dulcey just came up and licked my hand in a comforting way. She seems to sense our moods. Her tail waving is extremely cheering.

Sunday, October 19, 1902

Miss Wellington has started making plans for December. She told us today that our class will put on a Christmas play. The other students will be singing carols and giving recitations. But she wants us to act out a Christmas story. It is a nice one about a cobbler who wants Jesus to come to his house for supper. We have to start thinking about it because there will be costumes to make or find and parts to memorize. It seems early to start planning, but it is easy to see that Miss Wellington loves putting on plays and decorating and so on. The class is as pleased as she is.

Connor is going to play the part of the cobbler. I am going to be a beggar woman he helps. It is lovely.

Mother will make my costume. She says she is glad I am not an angel this time. Beggar women are much easier. No wings. In Montreal, our Sunday School dressed up as an angel choir and Olivia's wings were a big problem. They kept falling off.

—⧸⧹—

Friday, October 24, 1902

I couldn't write in my notebook the last few days. I had to write an essay for Miss Wellington. There are rules to writing an essay. I usually enjoy writing, but not this time. Maybe it was because I did not like the topic. It was supposed to be about the difference between Pity and Sympathy. Whatever I wrote sounded dull.

Monday, October 27, 1902

Mrs. Mutton is teaching me to cook. Mostly I have enjoyed it, but this time it seemed like hard work. We were making Christmas puddings. By the time we were halfway through, I felt worn out. Last time, we had fun.

To tell you the truth, I am feeling limp lately. When I wake up, I just lie there and ache. And I start wanting to go to bed in the middle of the afternoon.

I haven't told Mother. I do hope I get over feeling this way. It is as though I am dragging a big burden along wherever I go, only the burden is myself.

Tuesday, October 28, 1902

Today it really feels like winter. Much colder for October than it was in Montreal. We have a lot of people coming for the next couple of days. I wish so many of them wouldn't decide to stay here at once. I don't suppose they ever think of the beds to be made and the food to prepare and the dishes we have to do. When there's a crowd of them, they have a fine time, but we are worked off our aching feet. And Aunt Susan says we have to keep smiling however irritating they are!

I do feel sick.

Wednesday, October 29, 1902

I don't feel like writing anything. I think I might be getting a cold. I hope I am wrong about this.

Friday, October 31, 1902

It's Hallowe'en but I'm in bed already and it is only half past eight. Yesterday Bird and I made Davy a jack-o'-lantern, which he loves. But tonight I can't do more. Maybe John will do one of the other pumpkins. There are four faceless ones lined up on the verandah. I feel as blank as they look.

Also my throat is really sore and I can hear a rattling in my chest. I am rumbling like Turtle Mountain. Bird has noticed, of course, but nobody else. She says I must tell Mother, or she will. Sometimes she is almost as pushy as Mary Ruth.

Saturday, November 1, 1902

I have such a sore throat that I am hoarse today and, of course, Mother did notice. So I am in bed with a strip of flannel wrapped around my throat and she is going to make me a mustard plaster. Bird is supposed to keep Davy away from me, but I think he might have already caught it. He is too quiet and he comes and leans against me. Bird tried to coax him away, but he just put his head down on my shoulder and started to whimper. She brought a picture book to show him, but he fell asleep before she'd turned the page.

Sunday, November 2, 1902

I do feel very sick, too sick to write. They've moved Davy in with Mother. My chest hurts when I take a deep breath. John told me to stop making a fuss over nothing. I wanted to hit him but I hadn't the strength. I think I heard Mother scolding him a few minutes later. Good!

Tuesday, November 11, 1902

I have something called bronchitis. I hope I will soon start getting better. I feel wretched. Even my pencil is too heavy to hold.

Monday, December 1, 1902

I am up at last. I have had bronchitis and then pneumonia. It was horrible. I thought I would never be me again. But today I can tell that I am starting to get over it. I still feel weak, but not as though I might die. I know I was being ridiculous, but I was scared I was going to perish like Beth in Little Women. I suppose I should fill in what I missed, but I just can't. I haven't the strength of a cobweb.

Tuesday, December 2, 1902

I went to school, but after lunch I fell asleep with my head on the desk. When he heard this, John said some people will do anything to get attention. I hate him.

Olivia whispered to me that as soon as I feel better, she has an idea of how we can punish him. I wonder what it is. She used to back him up every time. He seems more obnoxious lately and she seems nicer. It is mysterious.

It is so cold outside. The wind seems to blow right through the walls and windows. You can't put your nose out the door without your teeth chattering.

Wednesday, December 3, 1902

I am back at school. I got 100 on my Grammar test. I always know the right word to choose but often I don't know why. This time, I did. It could be that reading through the grammar rules helped. I never tried studying before.

I am doing fine in every other subject too, in spite of being so sick. Miss Wellington says it is because I am a true scholar. She also told me that I would have a well-furnished mind when I grew up

It will soon be time for the concert. I know all my lines.

After supper, while John was out with his pals, Olivia and I made him an apple-pie bed. That was her brilliant idea. Now I am in my own bed waiting to hear what will happen when he comes home.

Later

I fell asleep but John roared loudly enough to wake the dead. He put his big feet right through the short sheet! Aunt Susan and Mother were not pleased, but Olivia and I laughed until our stomachs ached.

That will teach him to make mean remarks about his sisters.

I told Connor what we had done and he doubled up laughing. He said his sisters had better not get any such ideas.

It was lovely being in cahoots with Olivia.

Thursday, December 4, 1902

Less than a month until Christmas. I am SO excited about it. It will be a very different Christmas, spent in a hotel. Mrs. Mutton is making carrot cake and lots of cookies too. She sings while she bakes. I think she knows the words to every Christmas carol.

When she does "Good King Wenceslas" she sings in a little high voice for the page and a big booming one for the king. It is great. I don't have a beautiful singing voice like my sister, but I sing for fun when I am in a singing mood and I don't let it worry me if I go flat sometimes.

Friday, December 5, 1902

We went sledding today down a slope at the foot of Turtle Mountain. Bird got very upset when she found out and made me promise not to do it again. I argued with her until I found there were other places we could go.

The Dutchman who does a lot of the outside work for the hotel loaned us wooden shoes to put out for Saint Nicholas tonight. There's a pair for me and one for Davy. The others are too grown up. I am so happy not to be old like them at Christmastime.

I am glad I don't have to actually wear wooden shoes. They hurt my toes. They make a great racket too when you walk in them. You couldn't sneak up on anyone.

Aunt Susan shut Dulcey in the house after we put the shoes out. There must be food going into them. Sweet-natured as she is, Mark's dog would help herself to our Saint Nicholas treats.

Saturday, December 6, 1902

There certainly was food. Dutch chocolate and sugar plums and some of Mrs. Mutton's cookies. The Dutchman sang us a Dutch song. I got a gingerbread girl. I like her.

Olivia said it wasn't fair that she and John didn't get treats, but Mother had a gingerbread girl put away for her and a boy for John, even though I think he's too old.

He gave a scornful sniff and bit the head right off. I can hardly bear to eat the head and I always leave it until last and then nibble it slowly. I suppose, if you are a gingerbread person, you might want to be gobbled rather than nibbled, but I can't force myself to do that.

Wednesday, December 10, 1902

Connor told me something today that puzzles me.

He and I stayed late at school to practise the play. When we were waiting for Mark to come and pick us up, he asked me why I had not told him I was adopted.

"I wasn't," I said.

He was surprised. He said my mother had told his mother that I was. Then he informed me his little sisters are adopted. When his mother found out that these two babies had been left orphans after an accident, she had adopted them. She said she knew it was the right thing to do when she saw their red hair. (Her hair is red but not like theirs.)

When we got home, I told Mother about Connor thinking I was adopted.

"His mother said you had told her so," I said.

Mother stared at me and then she laughed. "Well, she was mistaken if that is what she thought," she said. "We did talk about her adopting the little girls. Then we talked about my children, it is true. But she must have gotten confused. Don't say anything to her about it, Abby, or you might embarrass her."

Then she sent me off to help with supper.

But I keep thinking about it. I wonder how it would feel to be adopted. Lots of girls in books are orphans. It must be exciting wondering about your past.

Friday, December 12, 1902

Four days until the concert. I haven't time to write. The days are so full of celebration. And of course we still have to keep the hotel going.

Dulcey stole a whole fruitcake from the kitchen table and was extremely sick. Mrs. Mutton said it served her right. I bet D. thought it was worth it.

Bedtime

Mother read Dickens's *A Christmas Carol* aloud three evenings in a row. It is a grand story. It started with just Davy, Bird and her mother, Miss Wellington and me listening, but by the finish we had gathered a crowd. Mrs. Mutton cried and blew her nose like a trumpet. Davy thought it was incredibly funny — Mrs. Mutton's nose, not Scrooge.

Tony is still hanging around whispering to Olivia. I don't know what he says, of course, but she blushes and looks embarrassed and he laughs as though he thinks he is incredibly clever. When he speaks to Mother, he puts on an extra layer of manners, but you can tell he does not mean them. Mother is polite but cool. Olivia drags him away as fast as she can. She knows he is being fresh. She does her level best to keep him and Mother apart.

Wednesday, December 17, 1902

The Christmas concert was a great success! When we came to the end of the play, some of the men cheered and everyone stood up. Mother told me that it is called a "standing ovation." Aunt Susan even cried!

I got Mother a present I think she will like, but I am not telling her ahead of time the way I did when I was little. It is a stone heart. I took a locket I had off its chain and strung the heart on in its place. The chain looks like gold even though it isn't. The stone is so smooth and it has a beautiful pattern. I earned the money by making cookies and selling them at the Christmas Sing. Jeremiah took a box of them to the mine and sold them to the miners. They were so popular I had to bake more.

Olivia played and sang so beautifully. I was filled with pride. She looked lovely too. Tony came over but he had been drinking and he started getting loud and making threats. Uncle Martin told him to leave and not come back until he sobered up. A couple of the men from the mine made sure he left. Olivia was red as fire as they marched him out the door. Mother told Olivia that Tony is too old for her.

"You aren't even eighteen. Tony must be twenty-five if he's a day."

Olivia said, "He thinks I am very mature."

He's over eight years older than she is. I know about Uncle Martin throwing him out because I was coming back from the dining room when it happened. Once he was outside, Tony met up with some of his buddies and took off down the road.

Change the subject, Abby.

On the night of the concert, Connor tripped getting up the step to the stage, but I caught him. He was grateful. I wasn't going to put it in here, but it was so nice, the way he looked at me and whispered, "Thank you."

Saturday, December 20, 1902

Now we are busy decorating the hotel. The boys fetched home a gorgeous tree that they cut down themselves. We have popped corn and threaded it with cranberries into long strings that will look like snow when it is looped on the evergreen boughs. We cut strips of coloured paper too and pasted them together. And Mrs. Mutton made some special cookies for hanging — stars and Christmas stockings and holly.

I wish Father could see how special Christmas can be. I still can't understand why he hated it so.

Christmas Eve Morning
December 24, 1902

I made Davy a toy dog out of rags. I was going to give it button eyes, but Mother said Davy might chew them off. So I embroidered them instead. It did not look like any dog I had ever seen, but Davy is not critical. It will fit in the Christmas stocking Mother has made for him. The stockings he wears aren't big enough to hold presents.

When Uncle Martin and Aunt Susan went to Lethbridge, they came home with a toy train for him. It's a proper one with wheels and real little windows. It has a locomotive, a passenger car, a freight car and a caboose. I can hardly wait for him to see it. I'm sure he will love it.

John muttered that they had wasted their money because Davy would not know what to do with it, but he is wrong. Davy loves playing with toys even though he does it differently.

Christmas Eve

Davy is asleep at last and it is time to hang up our stockings. Aunt Susan made us hang one up for everyone in the family. They look magical hanging in a row waiting for Santa.

Mother says I must go to bed or Santa Claus won't come. You'd think I was Davy's age.

Christmas Night
December 25, 1902

Christmas Day has been perfect. Davy was entranced by all of it. I had to keep pulling his hands away from the ornaments because he does not know how to hold anything gently.

The train was miraculous to him. He lies on the

floor and pushes it back and forth, back and forth, making train whistle noises. Other children would grow bored after a while, but not Davy. He likes my rag dog too. It does make him laugh, but that is fine with me. It is a comical animal.

Olivia has a necklace Tony got her. Mother asked her where it came from and she said she saved up and got it for herself. I wish she hadn't lied to Mother. It makes me miserable.

In spite of what John said about minding my own business, I think I maybe should try to talk to Olivia about Tony. Arabella says he got her cousin in trouble and then left her cold. I am not sure what she meant exactly. She would not say anything more except that I should tell Olivia he was not worth wiping her shoes on.

I can't do it. I know she would just be furious at me, and we are getting along so much better now. I'll wait and see if she finds out from somebody else.

Bird can hardly wait to borrow the book I got. It is called *Glengarry Schooldays*. I am halfway through. It is about boys but it is a good story.

Tonight, after almost everyone had gone to bed, Mother, John, Olivia and I sat down together in the lounge for a glass of eggnog. We were quiet for a while and then Mother said, "Thank you for helping make this such a happy day."

We looked at her and even John smiled. She didn't need to explain. It was as though we were one person for a few moments. I never felt quite that way before. I wanted it never to end.

Boxing Day
December 26, 1902

Jeremiah came over last night with a little cameo pin for Olivia. She showed it to Mother right away. No need to lie about Jeremiah! If I ever have a sweetheart, I want him to be one I can talk about to Mother. Not that I will have a sweetheart. Not for years anyway.

1903

New Year's Day
January 1, 1903

The holidays were full of fun. Mother got me new boots for Christmas. They are wonderful. The leather is soft and there is lots of room for my toes to wiggle. My old ones really pinched and they had worn almost through in places. Mr. Thornley, the shoemaker, also brought the nicest little shoes he had made for Davy. He was a bit embarrassed, but he said his sister had told him the little fellow had started to walk and he thought Davy should have proper shoes like any other boy. I did not know he was measuring Davy's feet the day he dropped by and took him up onto his lap. Davy is extremely proud of the shoes. He struts — and falls over!

We finally made a snowman. We tried before but the snow wouldn't pack properly because it was too dry. Mrs. Mutton produced a battered felt hat for him to wear. She put it on him and tilted it so it looks rakish. Is that the right word?

"It looks far better on him than it did on my old man," she said with a crack of laughter.

People went by and stopped to admire him. People here are so nice. Montreal was fine, but I know almost everybody in Frank. Well, not quite. There are a lot of men who arrive to work at the mine. Lots of them don't speak English but they have great smiles. Mark says the Finnish ones don't get along with the Italians. I wonder why. Maybe it is because they don't know the same language.

Mark took Dulcey out and introduced her to the snowman so she would know he was a friend and not attack him. As though sweet Dulcey would attack anyone!

It is now 1903. I wonder what this year will bring to our family. Last New Year's, I not only had no idea Father would die, but I did not know the town of Frank existed. Also, I did not know so many people who are close to me now. I had no idea I even had relatives in Alberta. And no best friend like Bird waiting for me.

The winter wind here blows hard and is so cold. It is like being run through with icicles. Uncle Martin drives us over to the schoolhouse in the sleigh when it is so cold our noses might freeze. The horse blows out great clouds of steam and Davy laughs and laughs.

When we walk where the road has been cleared, he holds my hand and marches partway in his new shoes. He slows us down but nobody minds. If we get too late, somebody scoops him up.

Saturday, January 3, 1903

I can hardly bear to write what has happened. We were all so happy. Then, last night, Olivia did not come home.

When we realized she was missing and looked all over for her, we found she had left a note saying she was going away with Tony, but that she would be back. She did not say she was going to marry him. Mother is sick with worry about her, and Uncle Martin went all the way to Lethbridge to search for her. He's still not back.

Why oh why did she go? I knew she should not trust Tony. Bird and I saw him out behind the stable kissing one of the kitchen girls while Olivia was playing the piano on New Year's Eve.

I wish I had told her even if it would have made her want to bite my head off. If only I had!

She's too young to get married. But her note did not say she meant to marry him. I know she has dreamed of having a real wedding with a bouquet and a bridal veil and everything. She and her friends used to sit around making wedding plans when we lived in Montreal.

Sunday, January 4, 1903

No word from Olivia. I cannot write about it. I never dreamed I could miss her so.

Monday, January 5, 1903

Olivia is home again! Uncle Martin heard that she had been seen in Pincher Creek and he went to look for her. She was there and he brought her safely home. Tony had left her, promising to come back for her. But he never came. He is a . . . a skunk! Worse than a skunk, because they don't mean to be cruel.

She has not said a word since they came in.

Tuesday night, January 6, 1903

At first Olivia shut herself up in the room she shares with Mother, but today she came out and went back to work in the kitchen. She seems smaller and much quieter somehow. When she finishes work, she mostly keeps to her room. I wish I knew how to comfort her.

I wonder if she is still hoping Tony will come back. I don't think she could be such a ninny. She never looks anyone in the eye now. She keeps her head down.

Arabella was home last night and heard Tony had been arrested for breaking into someone's house. She told everybody. Olivia just looked sick.

Wednesday, January 7, 1903

Davy was restless in the night so I woke up weary. Mother told Olivia to bring me a cup of cocoa. When she brought the cup in to me and I opened my eyes, I gave a shriek. The next second, Olivia gave a matching shriek. We each had spots like blisters all over our foreheads! When we shouted for Mother to come, she took one look, then said, in a voice of doom, "Chicken pox!"

Olivia could not believe she had missed seeing the spots on herself. I thought she must have brought them home from Pincher Creek, but Aunt Susan says it takes longer than that to catch them. She thinks one of the families who stayed here over Christmas probably had them. I remember those people — the two children acted sort of sickly — so she is probably right.

I just hope Olivia passed them on to Tony and he comes down with an enormous dose of them. Ours are multiplying and they are so itchy! They are everywhere — even inside our noses and on our bottoms! And we cannot show them off. The two of us are shut up in here together. Mother has removed Davy. And our spots are a Deep Dark Secret. We must not, MUST NOT, let it get out that there are chicken pox in Four Winds.

Luckily, John already had them when he was seven or eight. Mother had them, she thinks, when she was thirteen. Olivia and I do not care when they all had them. We just want to be rid of them. They itch! They are ugly! How we will manage to survive being shut up together for days and days, neither of us can imagine.

Mrs. Mutton says she'll pray for us. She also said we look like currant buns! That was unkind, but she baked us a pan full to make up for her cruelty. And hermit cookies too, which she knows are my favourites.

Thursday, January 8, 1903

We are going crazy in here. We read and we complain and we beg to be set free. We swear the spots are invisible. Mother and Aunt Susan open the door a crack and shake their heads. Jeremiah looked in the window and pushed a paper under the door, saying that we looked like leopards. And when he came back to the window, grinning, Olivia threw a cushion at him. But she was grinning too.

Friday, January 9, 1903

The school holidays are over.

Olivia and I are desperate for ways to pass the time. Today we wrote limericks.

Here's my best one.

> *A girl named Olivia is haughty.*
> *She's oftentimes dizzily dotty.*
> *But now she's in bed*
> *Where she's hidden her head*
> *To keep folks from guessing she's spotty.*

I think it is brilliant but Olivia is not impressed. Mother came in while I was writing and she says she thinks I should put this book away until my last scab falls off, in case it is contagious. So I can't even list my woes in your pages.

I wonder if my letters to Miss Radcliffe have given her spots.

Saturday, January 17, 1903

At last the pox are gone! We are free. We don't feel really well, but we look fine and that is what counts. People won't stay away from the hotel for fear of coming down with our disease.

Olivia has changed. Today Mother called and asked her to watch Davy while she washed my hair. I waited for her to refuse, but she didn't. She sat down on the floor and gave his train a little push. He stared at her and then he grinned his funny little grin and pushed it back with both his stubby hands and the two of them laughed. I could hardly believe it. It made me feel like singing the Hallelujah Chorus.

It also made me feel a bit jealous, to be quite honest. Only a bit.

Sunday, January 18, 1903

Olivia was having cramps and I had to take her place. Kitchen work is hard and repetitive. Scrubbing, peeling, doing dishes, stirring for hours. There is laughter along with the groaning, but my feet hurt. Come back, Olivia! HURRY!

Wednesday, January 28, 1903

I have fallen behind in my schoolwork. Olivia and I should have studied instead of writing poems. But I'm glad we didn't. We had fun and I'll soon catch up.

Saturday, January 31, 1903

Tomorrow will be February. Mother says time flies and she's right. I am sure it took longer when I was younger. There was something called "spare time" every day then. But nobody has heard of spare time here in Frank.

Monday, February 2, 1903

Davy has taught me to just sit and stare at the sky or a flower or Turtle Mountain in the snow. The clouds too. He tips his head back and waves to them. It makes me want to hug him.

Davy takes the time.

Wednesday, February 4, 1903

Davy has a cold. He often has them, but this time Mother says I must leave him home and go to school without him. It worries me. There are so many people milling around at the hotel. I wonder if she has noticed how much harder it is to keep track of him now he both crawls and walks. He wanders off and sometimes gets lost.

—∞—

Later

Davy was so happy to see me when I came home, but he is terribly snuffly with his cold. His poor little nose runs and is red as a cherry from being wiped.

Monday, February 9, 1903

Davy did get lost! I came home and waited for him to come trundling up to hug me but he didn't. I could not find him. I called his name and then began to look for him, but I could not find him *anywhere*.

Then Mabel, Arabella's sister, said he had been banging on the door so she had opened it to let him see it was too cold to play outside. Then someone called to her and she told him to come back in and went to see what they wanted. She was sure he had followed her in.

But he hadn't.

First we started searching the hotel. We looked everywhere, but there was no sign of him. If only he had answered when we called!

Then it dawned on me that Mabel had not actually seen him since she let him out and I got everyone to come outside and start seeking in the grounds. We have him back now. He was half frozen, just lying in the snow where he must have fallen.

Olivia was the one who found him. She tripped over him and she actually picked him up and lugged him back to the hotel. She said she could not leave him to come back for help because he had no warm coat and he was turning blue and not moving. He was stiff with cold. But when he saw her leaning over him, he smiled at her. Then he said, "O." When she told us this, she got tears in her eyes, remembering.

"He knew me," she said. "His foot was caught under a branch or something and he couldn't get free."

"Of course he knew you," Mother said and hugged her.

Getting him thawed out was painful for him. He sobbed. But he is in bed with me now, packed all around with hot-water bottles. He is warm as toast at the moment, but I am afraid he is going to be very ill. He just lies there wheezing. His eyes are shut but he is not asleep, and every so often he whimpers softly. Then he reaches out his hand and I take it in mine and kiss it and he smiles. But only a very weak smile. He seems far away. He is not exactly unconscious, but something like it. His breathing is uneven and hoarse. Dr. Malcolmson calls it "shallow." Everyone is worried about him. I did not dream so many people cared for him, but they keep dropping by to see how he is.

Olivia comes most of all. She stands and looks down at him and then she looks at me. When our eyes met last time, she whispered, "I'm sorry, Abby. I thought I didn't love him. But I do."

If he wakes up while she is here, he says, "O." It took us a while to know for sure that "O" stood for Olivia. He says so few words.

She loves it.

Wednesday, February 11, 1903

Davy has pneumonia. It is so strange that he did not get sick when I did, but now he is even sicker. The doctor has come several times — he lives just down the road. He listens to Davy's heart and then he shakes his head.

"His heart is having a hard go of it," he said. "I'm afraid he may not be able to pull through. I will help him all I can, but he's very ill."

I cannot imagine what life would be like without Davy. I won't go to school until he is better, whatever anyone says. So far, nobody has suggested I leave him. It is because I can get him to settle down. Whenever I go out of the room for even a minute, he starts to cry.

Wednesday, February 18, 1903

I have been so busy nursing Davy that I did not notice the days passing but, miracle of miracles, he is almost well again. And we are over halfway through February. He slept a lot, which allowed me time to do my schoolwork. So I'm not so far behind.

Jeremiah gave Olivia a beautiful valentine. I think his sister Polly helped him make it. It says, *Will you be my Queen of Hearts?*

Olivia was so delighted that I think maybe she is forgetting Tony. She is holding her head up and singing again. While she's working in the kitchen, she sings, and she's getting the others to join in now and then. Today they were belting out "Alouette!"

Yesterday I caught John helping himself to a fistful of sugar cubes from the dining room. He tried to worm his way out of explaining, but I got the story finally. He's made friends with Charlie, a horse at the mine, and he was taking the snack to him. He says he feels sorry for the horses who go into the dark mine. They live in there for long stretches, and they actually wear helmets to keep from being injured by falling chunks of coal. John looked sheepish when he told me there is something special about old Charlie.

I could not stop grinning after he had gone. Imagine my cold-hearted brother stealing sugar for a horse! It would not surprise me if Mark did such a thing, but John doing it is incredible.

Cousin Mark is smitten by a girl at last. Her name is Nancy and she's really nice. A bunch of them go riding together, leaving me to take charge of the telegrams. I never have to worry about remembering the Morse Code now — I'm getting really good at it.

Friday, February 20, 1903

Everyone went skating after school today. I wish I could whiz about like Miss Wellington. Olivia is good too. I skate on my ankle bones. Mother bundles Davy up and takes him out to watch for a few minutes. He smiles, but he is still so quiet, not back to his old self.

—∿—

Saturday, February 21, 1903

There are more people moving into Frank. It is interesting to meet people from so many places. They aren't all Canadians or even British. A family from Finland came last week. There are still only six hundred or so people, but they make quite a crowd when a bunch of them come to a Sing. I asked Bird why her people never come and she just looked at me. Then she said in a tight voice, "You know why, Abby."

And I do. I don't understand it, but they would not be made welcome at one. I think Bird would be if she came by herself, but not if she brought others.

She was not comfortable at school at first. Connor and I were her friends from the beginning, but it took the others a while. Since Christmas, though, everything sort of shifted. She was simply Bird, and we were just us. Maybe that is all there is to it. You have to get to know the ones who seem different to begin with and then they don't seem different any longer.

I want to go to her home some day, but I have not been invited. There are mixed-up feelings on both sides. But all that really matters is that Bird and I are best friends and we will make sure we keep it that way. I am missing her right now because she and her mother have gone home for the weekend.

Later

John sneaked me into the mine today when the shifts were changing to introduce me to Charlie. We had to be quick and whisper because it is supposed to be unlucky to let a female into a mine. But I had to go while Bird was away or she would be beside herself. Her grandfather has made her so terrified of being near Turtle Mountain.

Charlie is a nice horse. I understand why John likes him. But I was glad to get out of there.

I heard the rumbling clearly. I was right about it sounding ominous. Loose pieces of coal lay on the ground, and one piece fell just a few inches in front of me. It would not have hurt me — it was too small.

John actually laughed and said the mountain is doing them a favour by throwing coal down, but they still have to sort through the rubble. The bits that fall are not all coal. Some are useless rocks.

John admitted that it was harder work than he had expected. I hope Bird does not find out I went in there.

We have examinations coming up, so I must study. I'll be back to write in this notebook when they are over. Connor got me to help him learn the Grammar rules. I don't know why he needed help. He's really smart.

Sunday, March 1, 1903

We have had a rash of guests lately. It is not easy to find enough spare time for writing things down now. Partly it is because I have more friends. Partly it is because I must save time for Bird and Davy. And partly it is trying to go on doing well at school.

Spring is coming, though. I can hardly wait.

Monday, March 2, 1903

Bird goes on and on about Turtle Mountain being dangerous. It is frightening to listen to her. So I asked her to stop talking about it. I think I might have hurt her feelings. But when I told her about my nightmares, she understood. I had had a couple about the mountain falling down. I am sure it could not really happen, whatever Bird's grandfather thinks, but I hate those dreams. I wake up in a cold sweat. Bird confessed she has scary dreams too, but she has stopped talking about it.

Wednesday, March 4, 1903

Jeremiah is over here every evening now. Olivia's eyes grow bright and she welcomes him warmly these days. I remember how cold they were when we first came. She saw him differently. I imagine that he is much better looking to her now that she knows he adores her.

I thought something like this about the way we see Davy. He has always looked so endearing to me and to Mother. Yet Olivia told me long ago that looking at him gave her the creeps. I am sure that is no longer true. Yet it is not Davy who has changed. It is Olivia.

Must study.

Friday, March 6, 1903

Even though the Easter exams are a month off, Miss Wellington is giving us tests. I can't put everything aside while I study for them. There is housework to do and Davy to care for — even though he pays attention better now, so looking after him is easier. I'm not nearly as anxious about the tests as some of the others are. Still, I must go over my History notes.

Saturday, March 28, 1903

I cannot believe it, but March is almost over. We wrote the tests and I did well in everything. Uncle Martin says, if I do this well in the Easter exams, he will give me a fifty-cent piece as a reward. I have never had a reward for doing well in school before. Father did not believe in giving them even to John and Olivia. These days, whenever I am not in school or minding Davy, I am working the telegraph.

Maybe I should copy the Morse Code into this notebook. I will think about it.

More people come through here every day. I am waiting for spring. There are lots of snowflakes but no snowdrops! Aunt Susan promises me there will be lovely wildflowers in the mountains and I am eager to see them.

Sunday, March 29, 1903

Davy is still not as well as he was in the fall. But he is not in danger now. The doctor says I must be ready for him to be sick again though. His heart was damaged before he was born and has likely suffered more damage since.

"He's a great little fellow, but he'll not see old bones," Dr. Malcolmson said this afternoon.

Davy laughed and punched him on the leg, as though he understood what the doctor had said and he was proving him wrong. Dr. M. thought it was a great joke. "That's enough of that, young sir," he said, rubbing the spot. Then he picked Davy up and swung him around in the air. Davy kicked and shrieked with delight.

The doctor put him down and turned to me. "Don't feel sorry for him, Abby," he told me very gently. "His days may be short but they will be full of joy. After all, love is the ground he walks on."

I promised myself to remember what Dr. Malcolmson had said.

Tuesday, March 31, 1903

Jeremiah has proposed to Olivia! He waited until she turned eighteen and then he asked her.

Mother was flabbergasted but I wasn't. I saw it coming. And I think it will be good if Olivia does do it, because I believe Jeremiah truly loves her. He is someone she could trust. Mary Ruth thinks so, and so does Polly. She says Olivia is as beautiful as an angel. I suppose she is. Well, I know she is really pretty. It is only envy that makes me not admit it.

I wonder if she will have a white dress with a lace veil. She has always dreamed of herself dressed in one. I have seen her gaze at pictures of brides in magazines and stare at them in shop windows.

They want to marry quickly. Olivia thinks May Day would be perfect. But I don't think she can be ready that soon. When I began this book, almost a year ago, little did I think that I would be living in Alberta and, in less than a year, Olivia would be engaged to be married to a boy none of us had ever heard of.

Mother is convinced they should wait. When we were alone, however, I asked her to consider what might happen if another Tony shows up. Mother gave a shudder and then stared at me as though she were thinking my words over. I waited. Finally she admitted that I might be right.

"You are a very sensible girl, Abby," she said.

It is funny. Heroines in books are never called "sensible," but I think I like it. Mother's calling me sensible that way gave me a warm feeling inside.

Wednesday, April 1, 1903

Today was April Fool's Day. I tricked Mother. I told her what was left of the snow had all melted away in the night.

She went to the window and pulled the curtain back.

"My heavens, you're right, Abby," she said.

I ran to look and as I came up behind her, she swung around and said, "April Fool yourself, Miss."

You can't tell your mother not to be a smart aleck, but I was tempted.

Friday, April 3, 1903

Olivia has asked me to be her bridesmaid! I was shocked. I could feel my mouth fall open. She laughed at my stunned look.

"I know, little sister," she said. "You and I were never close before Father died. I think perhaps I saw too many things through his eyes. Mother told me so before we left Montreal, and I didn't know what she meant, but now I think she was right."

I stared at her and tried to believe what I was hearing. Then she took a deep breath and went on.

"It changes you when you're working in a kitchen and hearing other women's troubles and playing the piano and seeing people start to cry when you sing something that touches their hearts. I think my heart was hurt by Tony and that changed something in me too. And Davy calling me 'O' . . . and Jeremiah's love."

She smiled when she said his name and then made herself turn the smile toward me.

"Well, Abby, what do you say?" she asked very softly.

I was goggle-eyed still and she grinned. Then she went on. "I know now that you are my sister, no matter what anyone says, and I want you to walk up the aisle with me at my wedding."

I had never heard her make such a long speech. She grew flushed while she was speaking and twisted her hands together. Suddenly I knew that whatever had been wrong between us was over and done with. I felt filled with joy and I beamed at her. I couldn't help it.

"I would be honoured," I told her.

Then my sister put her hands over her face and burst into tears. She stammered, "I was sure you would say no."

I jumped up and hugged her. I knew that I had grown closer to her too since we came west. And since we had chicken pox together!

And I believe she was right about it having something to do with Father. I still don't understand why, but he made me feel as if I was somehow different. Mother never shut me out, but Father did. Oh, I am not making sense. The wonder is that everything is all right now.

Saturday, April 4, 1903

Everyone talks about the wedding. Olivia is going to make the dresses herself, with the women who work at the hotel helping. They do a lot of sewing in their free time.

She is going to ask Mary Ruth to be a bridesmaid too. And maybe Polly will be a flower girl.

My oh my! What an amazing thing! It feels like a

chinook blew through. They talk a lot about chinooks here. They are a wind of spring that comes blowing through early, like a preview of the warm-weather days ahead. You wake up and things are melting all around. Then, in a few days, the winter comes back. I wish it would happen, but I think it is too late now.

Sunday, April 5, 1903

Aunt Susan broke it to us that we are going to be spring cleaning this week to have the place shining clean for Easter. Miss Wellington says I can write my examinations in the morning and come home at noon to lend a hand. I have a feeling I am not going to enjoy the next few days.

Monday, April 6, 1903

We have started the horrible spring cleaning of the hotel. It is an enormous, exhausting job. We have to wash everything and whitewash or paint the walls and ceilings. There is a lot of smoke from all the hearth-fires and coal stoves and everything grows dingy and smudged by the time spring arrives. There are a million rugs to beat. Mark helps sometimes, although he is not keen on the job. We are saving goose down to fill the pillows. The ticks have to wait until summer, of course, when there is fresh straw to stuff them with. But there are floors and floors and floors to wash.

Aunt Susan goes around after us to check we aren't skimping the corners. We also must move the furniture out from the walls and clean behind and underneath. When it's warmer, we will wash the windows.

Writing my examinations is pure pleasure.

Tuesday, April 7, 1903

I never thought of washing picture frames until Aunt Susan took one down this morning and ran her finger along the top. It came away black with dust. Too bad she checked.

When it is done, I think it will be lovely and fresh, but I wish it was done already. I hope it NEVER gets this dirty again. I get so tired of it never ending.

Wednesday, April 8, 1903

We are getting there. Many hands do make light work. Lighter anyway. And everybody has pitched in. When a job is done, it does feel very fine. There are just far too many jobs.

I want to read a book. I feel as though I haven't read one for years.

Thursday, April 9, 1903

Aunt Susan says the end is in sight. Hurrah! If only she is right.

Davy spilled a bag of sugar on the kitchen floor today just after I got through washing it. Don't ask me how. But I confess that I wanted to kill my darling little brother. Sugar is not easy to wash up. Too sticky.

It was even in my ears by the time I had finished doing the job all over again.

Now March is past, we will hope that the wind does not blow so ceaselessly and hard. It would help to keep the place from getting so grimy. The gales that roared through in March were almost like hurricanes.

Good Friday
April 10, 1903

The hotel is spotless! There's no school today. Bird does not come to school anymore. Davy is so much quieter since he was ill. He sleeps a lot and does not need someone keeping an eye on him every minute. I miss her. I miss him too.

But I am getting to be friends with Mary Ruth and Polly. I love Polly and I like Mary Ruth more than I used to, even though she is sometimes a bit mean to Bird.

Saturday, April 11, 1903

Uncle Martin gave me my fifty-cent piece this morning. I did do well in the exams, but I thought he had forgotten.

The wedding plans are galloping forward. Everyone is excited and takes part. Mrs. Mutton is planning to bake a tall cake with four or five layers and decorate it with roses — she learned how to make them when she lived in Calgary.

Olivia positively shines. And Mother has stopped

wondering if they should wait. She told me privately that any man who could waken up the goodness in Olivia, the way Jeremiah has done, deserves her. It is true. I wonder what made her so distant before. Maybe she was trying too hard to live up to Father's praises.

That made me remember something she said that I don't understand: "You are my sister, whatever anyone says."

It was something like that. What could anyone have said? Of course I am her sister.

April 12, 1903

Easter Sunday. When I woke up this morning, there, lying on the chair in all its glory, was a new dress. Mother must have stayed up half the night to get it finished in time! It is so beautiful. She said Mrs. Mutton had helped, but Mrs. Mutton said she had done very little. I wore it to church and felt proud as a peacock. I kept opening up my coat as though I was too hot, but really to show off my glorious garment. I felt like one of the lilies of the field.

When we sang all the Hallelujahs, I felt we were singing about my dress. I am not a bit like Elsie Dinsmore, that is for sure. She's in a book I started to read but could not finish. She was such a goody-goody. She got a new dress but would not wear it to church in case it took her mind off the sermon.

For a book to be good, the people in the story must be real. Elsie is NOT.

Aunt Susan said I looked absolutely lovely in my new frock. I say dress, not frock. Mother smiled and smiled. I smiled and smiled back.

Every time I twirl and make my skirt stand out, I feel spectacular. Until now, almost every dress I have owned has been sensible looking and usually came to me as a hand-me-down. It is such a change to wear a really beautiful dress nobody else has ever worn, a dress made especially for me!

Easter Monday
April 13, 1903

Finally, the spring cleaning is over, the Easter holidays have begun and I have a new book to read. It is by Charles Dickens and it is wonderfully fat. It is not a children's book, although it starts with the hero a little boy. I won't clean and I won't write in this notebook. I am going to READ all day long. I've already started and it has made me cry. Poor little David.

Monday, April 20, 1903

I finished *David Copperfield*. I skipped a bit but how I did love it.

April is more than half over. Mary Ruth has invited me to come home with her for the night of her birthday. I don't like leaving Davy, but Mother says she'll sleep in my bed and he'll be fine. Her birthday is on April 28, which is a Tuesday. I know it is silly, but I feel homesick just thinking of going. I know

Mary Ruth and Jeremiah and Polly, but I don't know the others.

John is bunking in with Jeremiah at the stable sometimes now, so he is nearer the mine and can sleep a little later in the morning. I have made up my mind to talk to him once more about finding a job somewhere else.

He will be angry if I bring it up again, but I keep hearing more about coal falling down on the ground and the men don't have to dig it out but just shovel the loose stuff up. They laugh about this as though it is a great joke. John told us again that they claim the mountain is doing them a favour.

But why is the coal falling that way? I know nothing about mining, of course, but it still worries me, probably partly because of what Bird's grandfather says. She keeps telling me that he sometimes gets warnings — Miss Radcliffe would probably call them premonitions — and that sometimes they come true. What if he's right? What if the whole roof came down at once while John was standing underneath?

I know John would make fun of me for asking him to get a different job, but I can't help worrying.

Friday, April 24, 1903

I had a great shock today. It came when I tried to talk John out of going to work at the mine. He told me it was none of my affair, and no matter what I said, he wouldn't listen. "I am your sister — " I began.

"You are *not*," he burst out. "You are no relation to me at all."

I stared at him and he half-shouted out a story, one that he must have been wanting to tell me for years. I could not believe it. I still don't, even though I can tell he is certain it is true. I wanted to go straight to Mother, but I couldn't. If it is true, she surely would have told me long ago.

He blurted out that Grandpa found me abandoned on a dock in Montreal. Nobody seemed to know who I was. When Grandpa could not track down anybody who I belonged to, he carried me home to Mother. What John said was unbelievable, and yet it fitted with the words I had heard Uncle Martin say to Aunt Susan — that his father had brought a child home to Mother.

"But . . . Mother would have said something," I told John.

He had lowered his voice but he kept talking a mile a minute. "Your family probably died of cholera on one of the ships that came from Ireland or maybe England."

When I said it was not true, he glared at me. "I am not lying," he insisted.

The words kept pouring out of him as though they had been shut up behind a dam and I had finally let them out.

"I remember you coming. Father was away but Mother told us you were to be our sister. When

Father came home, he was angry about her taking you in. I don't know why exactly. But Grandpa took Mother's side and you stayed. Father wouldn't talk about it after a while and he made Olivia and me keep quiet about Grandpa finding you."

"Why?" I demanded.

John was getting hot and bothered and he admitted he didn't know.

"Anyway, you are not my real sister and that is that," John snapped at me. "Now let me out of here."

I stood stock still, too shocked to move or speak again. John had turned away so he need not face me. He was breathing hard. I could see drops of sweat on his forehead. I knew he wanted to escape, but I was between him and the door and I would not let him pass.

"Why didn't you tell me before?" I whispered at last.

"Father made me promise not to. He said I must let Mother tell you," he mumbled.

I wanted to ask why he had gone against Father's wishes now, but I knew the answer. He had held back then because he was afraid of Father. But now Father was gone and he was so mad at me that the whole story just burst out.

I knew, suddenly, that John had tried to make Mother tell, but she must have refused.

Why?

He started to shove me aside and then, all at once,

he said, "Don't tell her, Abby. Please, don't . . . "

But he knew he could not make me keep silent about this when he had been the one to break that silence in the first place. When I didn't answer, he stormed out of the room without another word.

I have not told her though, not yet. I must get it clear in my head.

I still would not believe him, except that I have a memory of my own that John knows nothing about. It is a memory I have never understood. When I have had time to think, it might fit in somehow and make sense.

If it does, I'll write it in this book.

Saturday, April 25, 1903

I need to think about all John told me, but I keep being interrupted. Mother caught me standing staring into space and asked me if I was feeling well. I said I felt fine. But it wasn't true.

I longed to burst out at her, "Who am I? Is Abby my real name? Is my birthday really in September?"

But whenever I made up my mind to talk, my tongue seemed to stick to the roof of my mouth.

When I do ask her, what will she do? She wouldn't send me away. I can't believe she would do such a cruel thing. I can still hear her saying, the morning Father died, "I knew I couldn't do without you, Abby."

Yet just thinking about it makes me feel cold right

to the marrow of my bones. Oh, why did John have to break his word and spill it all out?

Bedtime

I have gone to bed early. Davy is asleep. I have thought over that long-ago memory. Over the years since, I had come to believe what had taken place was a fairy story, not a memory at all. I have always liked dreaming up stories about myself as a gypsy or a queen or even a horse. But this was no such make-believe story. I believe it is a true memory of what happened, long ago, to the little girl I was, a lost and frightened little girl, needing Mother. I lay in bed and relived that day.

I had been wrapped in a thick, dark blanket that came up so high I could not see over it. I was carried up steps into a house by someone. If John and Uncle Martin are right, it must have been Grandpa. I think he said something like, "My girl needs you."

Then a child's voice demanded, "Who is that?"

The man pulled the edge of the blanket down and I saw a sharp-eyed boy staring up at me.

"I've brought you a little sister," the man told him. "Run and get your mother."

"But I don't want another sister," the boy said.

Then he ran away.

That's all I remember. But was that Grandpa bringing me to Mother? And was the boy John? I wonder if he remembers saying he did not want another sister.

But Mother wanted me. I can still feel her arms wrapping around me, holding me close. I remember that hug and nothing more.

I must try to sleep.

But how can I?

Sunday, April 26, 1903

Today everything goes on as usual. I feel like a stranger to myself, but nobody notices. John is keeping out of my way. Olivia is so caught up with planning her wedding. I don't want to trouble her.

But I have lost myself and don't know what to do next. I wish Bird was here to help.

Monday, April 27, 1903

I long to run away from my thoughts. I need to ask Mother about what really happened, but I am afraid to start. I have never been afraid to ask her anything before.

Mrs. Mutton asked me what was wrong. When I muttered "Nothing," she shook her head and went back to her work. She's the only one to notice.

Tuesday, April 28, 1903

Davy gave me a tight hug this morning. He's like Dulcey. He knows when I need cheering up.

This is the night I am supposed to go to Mary Ruth's birthday celebration. It was so warm the last few days but it has suddenly turned very cold. I know that the weather has nothing to do with my wanting to stay home tonight. I just do not think I can bear to leave at the moment. That might not make sense to anyone but myself, yet I feel as though I must stay near Mother right now. What if she should vanish before I have made myself talk with her about what happened to us long ago? Yet I can't seem to begin. I don't understand myself. According to John, I was lost and then rescued. What if I went away and got lost again before I could get back?

Bird should be here any minute. I think I will tell her what John told me. I need to spill it all out to somebody who will help me get it straight. If it is true, it feels like a load too heavy for me to lift.

Later

I have told Bird everything. She is a wonderful listener. She became very serious and thoughtful. She was quiet until I got to the end, not once butting in or looking disbelieving. Then she said it was a strange story but she believed it, and she was certain I must ask my mother to explain it all.

"I loved Grandpa a lot," I said slowly, remembering those long-ago times. "He died when I was five. I think. My grandma died before I was old enough to know her. He always took me on his knees and told me over and over that I was his granddaughter and I must never forget it. I promised I wouldn't, but I did not really know what he was talking about."

When I told Bird this, she smiled. "You mustn't forget," she said. "And you must not go to Mary Ruth's tonight. Just before I left home, I told Grandfather you were going over there and he got very upset. He told me to tell the people here that he fears the mountain is ready to fall. He would not say anything more, but he was shaking. He made me promise not to let you go. I said I would do my best, but he said that was not good enough."

"Did you promise?" I asked her. I did not see how she could have promised.

She stared at me and her eyes looked bigger than usual.

"Yes. I had to," she said. "Or he would not have let me come."

"But what will I tell Mary Ruth?" I asked her.

We were trying to decide this when Mary Ruth herself arrived. She made a rude face when she saw Bird.

"Happy birthday," I started, but she interrupted.

"Come on, Abby," she said, as though Bird was not standing there. "My father says to be quick because he must get back."

"I'm not coming," I told her. I could feel myself blushing because I could not think how to explain. She would not give a hoot about what Bird's grandfather said. I don't understand it, but she seems to dislike anyone who is not white.

"Why ever not?" she demanded. She practically

shouted the words and her eyes flashed. "You said you would."

"I know," I admitted. "I can't explain why. I am sorry. Why don't you stay here tonight instead?"

She did not answer, she just slammed out of the room and ran back to where her father waited. It wasn't so very far to her place. Mother says nothing is far in Frank.

Even though we did not come to blows, I knew Mary Ruth was furious. She would blame Bird for keeping me from going with her. That was not true, but I could see how it looked.

"Let's try persuading her," Bird said, starting to run after the pair of them.

We caught up with Mary Ruth, and Bird talked fast, saying she really wished Mary Ruth would stay at the hotel tonight. She began to tell Mary Ruth about her what her grandfather had said.

Mary Ruth glared at her. "What your people say about the mountain is pure rubbish," she yelled. Then she stomped away through the mist.

While we stood watching them go, Bird's mother came to tell us that she was staying at the hotel to help out, because word had come that extra guests were expected. Bird was to stay too.

I don't think she could have made Bird leave me then, but neither of us said so. Having her there was a comfort. For one thing, it meant I could wait another day at least before I would have to ask Mother about

Grandpa's finding me. I wanted to think out what to say.

Now I have gone into Davy's and my room to try to settle down. He's not here. Mother said she would bring him later. I think she saw how upset I am.

Bird is going to sleep in here with me, but she is doing something with her mother first. I am glad I had a chance to write down what happened with Mary Ruth before Bird came. I hope I didn't hurt Mary Ruth's feelings.

I wish she would not be so nasty to Bird. Jeremiah and Polly aren't at all like that. I wonder what makes people from the same family think so differently. Well, I suppose I know some of it. I just have to remember the way Father was toward Davy.

After midnight

Bird has gone to sleep at last. We talked and talked and then we got up and sneaked into the kitchen and made ourselves what boarding school stories call a "midnight snack." Davy slept through it all but then, just as Bird fell sound asleep, and I was about to do the same, he woke and started to cry. It was not his usual crying. He sounded scared. And he wouldn't stop. I was afraid he would wake Bird, but she was dead to the world.

I could not find anything wrong with him, so I just rocked him and sang. It was not easy at first, since I kept drifting off. But once he knocked the last scrap of sleep out of me, he hushed, smiled and began to snore again. I wanted to smack him because I am now wide awake. I am writing this while I wait to grow drowsy again.

Thursday night, April 30, 1903

Turtle Mountain has fallen! It happened before dawn on Wednesday morning, the night Bird stayed over.

I can't write more now. We don't know where John is. Mark is missing too. Mother and Aunt Susan are frantic and I can't stop crying.

Later

It has been almost two days since the Slide. I think I can put down some of it now, although I will never be able to tell the whole horror of what happened.

A strange sound woke me. The grandfather clock in the hallway chimed four o'clock. I almost fell back asleep and then came a sound like a thunder clap — only much louder. Just the one boom and then an eerie silence. Then there was a splintering, ripping sort of noise as though something enormous had run past the hotel, crushing everything as it went.

Bird gasped and sat bolt upright. Davy buried his face in my front. I patted his back, but I could not concentrate. We heard bedroom doors opening as people ran to look outside. But by then everything had grown still again.

"It must have been nothing," a man's voice said. "I'm going back to bed."

"No," Bird said in a thin, high voice. "It was Turtle Mountain walking. Grandfather said it would happen."

Her voice frightened me. I wrapped Davy in his quilt and reached to take her hand, but she pushed me away and stared through me as though I were invisible. The silence that came after the cannon blast was louder than the noise had been. I know that doesn't make sense but it is true. It echoed in our ears, the sound of silence. Then noise came flooding back.

A tidal wave of sounds.

I don't know how long we stayed there, frozen, not knowing what we were supposed to do. It felt like an hour but I suppose it was only minutes. Then I carried Davy out into the hall. Uncle Martin was there, hopping on one foot while he pulled on his trousers. I stared at him but he didn't explain. He just ordered me to go and see if there was a telegraph message coming in. I turned to the door and reached for the handle.

"Don't go out there, Abby!" Bird screamed, clutching at me. "You'll be killed!"

I shifted Davy so I could hold him with one arm, then I pulled the big door open a crack. I stood staring out into the darkness. Except it wasn't all dark. I peered out but what I saw made no sense. I felt as though I were sleepwalking and in a strange place I had never been.

My arms shook and I was afraid I would drop Davy, so I put him down on the floor. Then I just stood, waiting for someone to tell me what to do.

The air was filling with dust — gritty dust that smelled of smoke. I blinked hard, but I could not see anything clearly in the darkness.

Then Uncle Martin grabbed my shoulders and yanked me away from the door into the hall. His fingers had a grip like iron. I was already off balance so I toppled over backwards and landed half on top of Davy, sprawled on the floor.

It is still hard to even write this.

Inside me, a voice kept saying, "He was right." And I knew "he" was Bird's grandfather. The mountain had walked, just as he had said it would. And it had walked right over Frank.

Friday morning, May 1, 1903

I'm watching to see that Davy naps, so I have a little time to write. I'll start up where I broke off last night.

I crouched in the hall, choking partly with terror and partly because the air was thick with bits of dust. Everywhere people were coughing and fighting for breath. Davy wrapped his arms around my legs. He was screaming.

I got up and reached to get him. He wound his arms around my neck then and practically strangled me. He must have been terrified. In the few seconds

I had looked out the door, he and I had both seen a world we did not know. Fires seemed to be springing up on the other side of town. Some turned out to be only lanterns, but others were real fires.

People were screaming and running every which way. There were cries that must have been made by injured animals. Mostly horses. There was constant rumbling and crashing such as I had never heard before. I know now that it was great chunks of Turtle Mountain breaking loose and coming down, carrying tons of mud and rocks with them. The weight of sliding earth was crushing everything that got in the road. Parts of Frank were being buried or swept away while I stared out into the night.

I heard somebody shriek, "It's the end of the world!" I wondered if it might be true.

As the seconds passed, more and more voices joined in. Some called children's names. A few were children themselves crying.

It wasn't just the noise that was terrifying. Huge boulders came crashing past. Nothing was clear in the dark and yet the light shining out from the hotel windows showed flashes of things.

I began crying, which washed some of the grit out of my eyes. It is hard to know what to do when something so horrifying happens without warning.

The hotel's front hallway was soon jammed with people, many in their nightclothes. None of them knew what to do either. More and more people were pushing and shouting questions. Bird was close to me. I could hear her crying. I was beginning to feel my breath squeezed out of me and I could hear Davy struggling to get some air when Aunt Susan, using her elbows and boots, barged through to us and hauled us out of the crush. Bird hung on to her too. We tramped on people's feet but nobody was noticing.

Aunt Susan kept barging through whoever was in her way until we got to the foot of the stairs, where Mrs. Mutton was standing over a pail of water, handing out drinks to people who were about to faint. Mother was beside her, helping.

"Oh, Susan, you're wonderful," she said, doing her best to hug me and Davy. I leaned against her without speaking and did not even notice, at first, that I was squeezing Davy so hard that I was hurting him. When he whimpered, I loosened my grip and kissed him. Then I mopped my face on his nightshirt.

It was just then that Mother realized John had not come to tell us he was all right. Her face went white and she dropped the ladle. She said just one word, *John*, and suddenly I knew what she meant.

I can't write any more.

Saturday, May 2, 1903

There is too much to write all at once. I keep needing to find a drink of water because the inside of my mouth feels raw. Water helps, but not for long.

Mother pushed out through the crowd, Uncle

Martin leading the way. Bird ran down the hall and came back with my dress and boots.

"Here," she said. "Get these on." She sounded like a general.

I stripped off my torn nightgown and got dressed automatically, not caring that we were still out in the hall. Then I waited for Bird to tell me what to do next.

Later

John is wounded but safe, but there is so much to do. It is like living in an enormous jigsaw puzzle which has been dumped out of the box with no picture to tell you how to fit the bits back together. Except it is not just one jigsaw but a heap of them, all mixed up. And we are broken too. Many of us looked fine at first, but now we are finding out that parts of us are missing. I know that sounds crazy. But it is still true. Many people have hurts inside, hurts that will never heal.

I'll go on with this later.

Saturday night

The Premier of the North-West Territories was here today, Frederick Haultain. He says we must be evacuated. We will be going tomorrow. He is afraid there might be another landslide.

I read over what I have written so far. It sounds choppy. Perhaps I can tell it properly if I go more slowly. When I start writing, though, I start to tremble and my hand grows unsteady. I need to be by myself sometimes and that is hard to do. Right now, for instance, I hear Olivia calling me. I will return to my writing later, but it feels as though there was a landslide in my notebook.

Bedtime, but I can't sleep

Less than half of Frank is buried. It seems like more but it is just the southeastern edge, really. Mary Ruth is dead. Her whole family was killed in those two minutes. Jeremiah's parents and his younger brothers died. Polly was at a friend's house and she is still alive, but she was in a coma at first and, although she is conscious now, she does not speak yet. The doctor believes she will recover in time. I pray he is right.

Priscilla's family died and so did Jessie's. But the Ennis family are alive. Gladys, the baby, was found buried in mud and they thought she had died, but she is all right. Mrs. Ennis carried her body to the neighbours, thinking she was holding a corpse because Gladys was so still, but once they cleaned the mud off, they discovered she was just in shock. Mrs. Ennis says she cannot go on living in Frank though and they will be moving away.

So many are buried under tons of rock. I came home after we found John and Jeremiah. They are alive, but I can't tell about our finding them right now. I am too tired and the page keeps getting streaked with my tears.

Sunday, May 3, 1903

I will tell first about what happened to John and Jeremiah. The two of them were together and they got trapped in the wreckage of the livery stable where Jeremiah had gone to check on one of the horses. They were coming out when the Slide struck, and the stable itself was demolished. They would have been killed along with the horses if it had not been for the way one beam fell. It trapped them, but it also saved them from being crushed by falling chunks of the mountain and great boulders that landed on either side of them. At first they were unconscious, but when John came to, he found he could not move and neither could Jeremiah. The rocks and wood piled around them also hid them from sight. John told us he cried out for help, but in all the noise, nobody heard him.

Bird and I were searching for them as soon as Mother realized John hadn't come back to the hotel. She and Uncle Martin ran toward the mine, Bird and I toward the stable. We would never have spotted them if it had not been for Davy, though.

It gives me the shivers to think how we almost left Davy behind. Everyone was too busy to mind him, so we just had to bring him along. While we were staring around helplessly at the huge boulders and smashed buildings, Davy quietly toddled off on his own. It wasn't a safe place and Bird shouted to him to come back.

He didn't, of course. The two of us went after him, making our way through the piles of broken boards, smashed and heaped against each other. It was terrible because of the dead horses. There were bones sticking out. Oh, I can't describe it. I kept wanting to shut my eyes so I wouldn't see, but I couldn't, not if I wanted to find Davy or John.

Then, all at once, we did find Davy, hunkered down in a corner where the planks had formed a sort of rough cave. He was half hidden by the large beam and the boulders.

Then I heard John's voice from somewhere near, begging Davy not to leave him and then asking, "Where's Abby? Davy, where's Abby?" over and over again.

I scrambled through to Davy and saw him stroking someone's face. It was John, although he was hard to see in the shadows, and all covered with stone dust.

He and Jeremiah were both pinned down by that one huge beam. Only two big boulders that it rested on had saved them from being killed.

Dulcey had been with them, but I did not notice her body lying there until later. Thank goodness Davy did not see her.

I stayed with the boys while Bird went for help. John had gripped my hand and I could not leave him. Dr. Malcolmson's office was full of people but Bird made him come, and on the way, collected Olivia.

When Olivia reached us, she went down on her

knees in the dirt and kissed Jeremiah for all the world to see. She stayed with him while the boys were dug out and carried to the hospital and she has not left him yet.

It was not easy freeing the boys without increasing their injuries. John cried out, but luckily Jeremiah did not know what was happening until later. He had to have his left leg amputated. The bones were crushed and his leg could not be saved.

I can't bear to think about this. John's back was wounded. The fact that he was lying on the cuts helped a little to stop the blood from flowing. Otherwise he might have bled too much to recover. His collarbone was broken, but otherwise he will be all right when the fractures have had time to heal. Whenever I stop to think about it, I can't help weeping. It isn't just crying. Weeping comes from your heart.

The day after the Slide, I finally took in the truth about Mary Ruth's family. They had all perished when their house was buried under the mountain. When I realized I would have died with them if Bird had not made me stay home, I threw up. Bird's face paled but she managed not to vomit.

At last count, they say over seventy people have been killed. All seven of the row of small houses where the miners' families lived got flattened by the Slide. The houses are now buried under tons of stone. Uncle Martin says they will not be able to get the bodies out.

I forgot to say that while we were looking for John,

Mark showed up at the hotel, much to Aunt Susan's relief. He had been at Nancy's house and they had talked him into staying late. When he fell asleep on their couch, her mother said they should let him sleep till morning. Their place is at the far end of Frank from the hotel. At first Aunt Susan had made up her mind that Mark was buried under the Slide. When he walked in to the hotel, he looked stunned by all the wreckage he had seen. She probably looked stunned too, but with joy.

When I was in bed last night, I suddenly remembered Charlie, the horse John took treats to. I thought of him lying dead in the mine and I began to cry and could not stop. It is strange. I have heard such terrible things about people dying and have not fallen apart, and then just remembering Charlie broke my heart. I hope he died instantly and was not afraid or hurt.

We are going to be evacuated in the morning. They have brought boxcars for us to ride in, and we are to take whatever we will need in the next ten days or so with us. I will take this notebook.

Remember how I complained about spring cleaning? When we come back home, we are going to have to clean the whole hotel. I thought the spring cleaning we did was such a huge job. Cleaning up the mess left by the Slide will be one hundred times worse.

Yesterday I heard a woman say Frank will be a ghost town now. And it does feel that way sometimes, even though the Slide did not damage the whole town. Some of the people actually slept through it and did not know what had happened until daylight showed them. The landslide not only came down the mountain, it went right across the valley floor and a long way up the other side.

When I think of Mary Ruth and her family, I still begin to cry again. Mother gives us jobs to do. She thinks keeping busy helps. But inside each of us is an emptiness that won't go away.

Monday, May 4, 1903

We have been evacuated. Frank really is a ghost town at the moment. We are staying in the Mounties' barracks. It feels so strange. The authorities want to wait until they are sure there won't be another landslide.

At least, here, I have a little more time to write. No hotel chores to do.

Davy and I are together in a space which is more like a closet than a room. We share a single bed, which is small, but no worse than the berth on the train. It wasn't a bedroom, but they found there was enough room in it to put our cot and still shut the door. This way, if Davy grows noisy, nobody is disturbed. Davy is a bit disruptive. That is what Aunt Susan calls him. The rest of the family are in beds in the big room right outside the door. But I will be glad when we can move back into the hotel.

We are so lucky that the Slide missed us. We had broken windows, but no lasting damage except tons and tons of stone dust and dirt the four winds of Frank have spread around.

Today they brought John up here. He is still wrapped in bandages and must stay in bed. We have to change his dressings every day and he always asks for me to do them because I have a lighter touch. I know why this is. I learned to be gentle when I changed Davy or he would howl and kick. John does not struggle and we don't talk much. But we understand each other.

Tuesday, May 5, 1903

Today John asked me if I realized we had played a part in history. He thinks that there might never have been such a huge disaster before in Canada. He heard some men discussing it when he was at Dr. Malcolmson's and that is what they thought.

I suppose he is right. But aren't ordinary days, when no mountains walk, also history? I believe history has peaceful days as well as disasters. It is just that nobody writes those days down.

Wednesday, May 6, 1903

Today when I was bandaging John's back and shoulder, he told me he had confessed to Mother that he broke his promise and let me know about how I came into the family.

I asked him what she said. He shook his head and whispered, "Nothing. She looked at me and then she walked away without a word." He said he felt lower than a worm.

"Forget it," I told him.

When he stared up at me and began to talk about it again, I got up and walked away, just like Mother. I don't want to think about it right now. Someday soon I will have to face it, I know, but I must get past the shock of the Slide first.

Bird says I will find the strength I need, but her family took her home soon after the Slide, so I don't have her to bolster me up. I do miss her in this strange place.

Thursday, May 7, 1903

Mark told us such a story today. Mr. Mackenzie, one of the miners who survived, came to where a group of men were gathered and started talking in a really loud voice — he was nearly deafened by the mountain falling. Quite a few people had trouble hearing afterward.

Mr. Mackenzie was one of the seventeen miners trapped underground when the Slide happened. It was pitch black and the air was filled with stone dust.

Tons of rock had sealed off the mine entrance. The men were trapped and could not find an opening to get out. Luckily they had their picks and chisels with them. They decided to try to dig out through the coal seam.

They got up on one another's shoulders and began

to chop at it with their picks. It got harder and harder to breathe. They tried, at first, to sing to keep their spirits up, but they could not risk running out of oxygen. Some gave up and slumped down, and some cried. Then Mr. Mackenzie said they should try once more, and all at once his pick broke through and light streamed in. Light and fresh air!

The miners cheered and hugged each other, even though the hole was clearly too small for them to squeeze through. The fresh air coming in gave them hope and strength. They finally cut through in another place.

"One minute we could not breathe and the next we were whooping with joy," he said.

When I heard Mr. Mackenzie's story, I shared his joy. Yet I could not forget all the others who did not get out but are buried under tons of stone. Just thinking about it makes me feel sick even now. It helps if I make myself think about the moment when Mr. Mackenzie's pick broke through into daylight.

Bedtime

Davy is asleep but I am too restless, so I'll write a little more.

Olivia never left Jeremiah's side until they got the beam off and carried him out to freedom. When she came home, she was not a girl anymore. She was a woman. And her voice had changed. It was deeper and there were no giggles left in it. Her face, too, had become a woman's. I can't explain, but if I had Before and After pictures, you would be able to see the difference.

She was always pretty. Now she is beautiful.

Olivia stayed at Dr. Malcolmson's until we were evacuated. They brought Jeremiah up here to the barracks, and she is never far from his bedside. He's so brave! What with losing most of his family and worrying about Polly and wondering how he will manage with only one leg. I can't see how he can bear the days but he actually jokes when he is conscious.

He is in a lot of pain, so he is given laudanum. John spends time with him whenever Olivia is helping with other patients.

It is amazing though. There are only a few survivors who were seriously injured by the Slide. Doctors and nurses came, expecting there would be many wounded people needing to be cared for, but there weren't.

I should get back to telling some of the other things that happened the night Turtle Mountain walked. I think that is not the right word to use, but no word quite fits. Most of the mountain is still there, looming over the town, but with one side all tumbled down.

They're saying that millions of tons of rock came down on the mine site. And there are still gigantic blocks of stone standing up like monuments, and hundreds of smaller broken-off pieces and thousands of even smaller bits. The largest rocks are taller than a house.

Friday, May 8, 1903

I want to write down some of the other stories about people. Stories are better than facts about how many tons of stone hurtled down.

I could start with the most astounding of all. The Leitches' little girl, Marian, was asleep in her bed when the Slide hit. Somehow the blast sent her flying through the window, leaving behind their flattened house. Six people in her family were killed but two of her sisters survived. They say she landed on a pile of hay. I am not quite sure how it looked with her perched on the hay, but it is incredible. When people found her, she wasn't crying or hurt, but still very much alive.

Someone told Aunt Susan that when they first spotted her, she was actually smiling. She and Gladys Ennis are both so little and yet they both lived through the Frank Slide!

Then there is Mr. Choquette, who stopped the express train and saved the lives of all the passengers. He and another man realized there was no way to warn the incoming train's engineer, with the telegraph lines to the east being down and the railway tracks buried under a mass of fallen rocks. It must have seemed that getting word through was impossible. But Mr. Choquette started clambering over the rocks in the darkness. Thinking of the people on the incoming train, asleep and being carried to their deaths, was so terrible that he had to try.

The other man could not make it through, but

Mr. Chouquette kept struggling on and finally he got to where he could wave his arms to warn the engineer to put on the brakes in time. Mr. Choquette said he almost gave up, but he knew passengers were coming toward Frank with no idea what had happened up the track. It only took about half an hour, but he said when he realized that, he could not believe it. He thought he had struggled on over the rocks forever.

It gives me the shivers to think of those travellers peacefully sleeping as the express train chugged along, carrying them through the darkness to their death. When I first learned about heroes, I wondered if I would ever meet one. Well, now I know the answer. I have met one. He is Mr. Choquette.

Later

I wrote a letter to Miss Radcliffe today. I don't know how it will reach her, with the rail lines still buried. But she must be filled with worry about us, so I wrote to tell her we are all fine. I didn't want to worry her about John's hurt back. I also told her that Olivia and Jeremiah are engaged.

I get so tired of writing everything down, but somehow I feel bound to do it even though I'm kept busy tending to Davy or helping with John. I feel like a historian.

There are other stories of lucky escapes.

John Thornley, the shoemaker who resoled my

boots and made Davy his first shoes, persuaded his sister Ellen to stay overnight at the Frank Hotel with him. If he hadn't, she would have gone home and died with the rest of their family. He told Aunt Susan that he has no idea why he talked her into staying over. He believes there must be a reason why he and his sister were spared while the rest of their family perished. He went on about it for so long that Aunt Susan finally told him to stop fretting — he would learn the answer in God's good time. She sounded so practical that it calmed him down.

But why did Mary Ruth and the rest of Jeremiah's family have to die? I wanted to shout this question at Aunt Susan. The great slabs of the mountain that still stand are too big to be moved, but they stand as reminders of the tragedy. At last count, seventy-six people have been killed, and dozens are still missing. Whole families died in less than two minutes.

Babies. I can't bear to remember the babies. Eleven children died. Aunt Susan says it is a comfort to realize that not one of them knew anything was wrong before they died, since it was all over in seconds. I am not comforted by this.

In the first days after the Slide, I tried to stay close to Mother. I knew such a disaster could not happen again, but just in case I was wrong, I did not want to be caught some place where I could not reach her.

—◊—

Bedtime

They say we will be returning to town tomorrow or maybe the next day. I will be so glad to be home again even though we will have to face the wreckage around us.

So much else has changed since the day I first wrote in this notebook. Olivia knows now that she actually loves Davy, although she still is squeamish about keeping him clean. And she's engaged to Jeremiah. He's learning to use crutches so that he can walk down the aisle with his new wife at their wedding.

Polly has spoken a few words at last. She is still weak and gets things muddled up sometimes. Still, if she is well enough, she will be the flower girl.

Saturday, May 9, 1903

As our world slowly returns to normal, I find my mind going back to what John let out about the beginning of my life. I must ask Mother to tell me whatever she can about the day I was brought to her. I must. Yet I cannot seem to do it. Bringing up something that happened such a long time ago is not easy. I can't think how to start. So I am waiting. I feel that I will know when the time comes.

Sunday, May 10, 1903

We are going home today. Bird and her mother will be coming back. I am so glad to be going home.

Later

Bird and her mother were already here when we got to the hotel. As soon as we were alone, Bird asked what had happened when I spoke to Mother about my being found long ago. When I admitted that I still had not asked, she was furious at me and told me that I should trust my mother. Anyway, she made me promise to ask her about it tomorrow. When I think about doing it, I feel afraid. No, that isn't right. But anxious.

I wish I had not promised.

Bedtime

I did it! I coaxed Mother to come out for a walk and when we were far enough from the hotel not to be interrupted, I took a deep breath and plunged in.

"John told me about Grandpa finding me and bringing me to you. Why didn't you tell me? What made you decide to keep me?"

Mother stood stock still for a second. Then she took my hand and kept walking without speaking. I thought maybe she was never going to tell me anything. But finally she said, "I know I should have talked to you about it long ago, Abby, but when I was free to do so, it was never the right moment."

She stopped to take a breath and I thought I would burst. But I managed to keep still until she went on.

"It was simple, really," she said, looking at me and then away. "From the moment my father put you

164

into my arms, I loved you. And I couldn't bear to let you go."

She stopped speaking, searching for the right words again. I longed to shower her with questions, but I bit them back. Then she stopped walking and turned to face me.

She said that Father was off on a job when Grandpa brought me, so she had several days with me before Father came home. "By then, you were so dear to my heart that I could not give you up whatever he said," Mother finished.

She hesitated.

"What did he say?" I prompted her.

"He was horrified that I had accepted a stray baby into our home without his consent," she said. "He did his best to convince me that keeping you would somehow harm our own children, and he wanted to take you to a foundlings' home, but I would not do it." She explained that the only one she had seen was a bleak place, not fit for any child.

She stopped talking long enough to blow her nose, but I just kept still. I was learning my story at last and I wanted to hear more.

"You needed me so," she went on at last. "To begin with, you clung to me like someone who is drowning, and in the night, you cried out with nightmares. You were also terribly thin and weak. So, when your father finished having his say, I insisted we must look after you until you recovered."

Then she said, in a voice close to a whisper, "You did need me, but the truth is that *I* needed you, Abby. I was very lonely at that time . . . "

She broke off again and I longed to ask why. But at last she went on to tell me more about her battle with Father, and how he finally agreed she could keep me on condition that we never tell anyone how Grandpa found me, or even talk about it at home.

At that, my eyes burned with tears I knew would soon be rolling down my face. But I did not just want comforting. I wanted answers. She drew me over to one of the boulders left by the landslide and we sat down side by side.

She said that long before I arrived, she and Father had grown apart. He believed Mother was too soft with Olivia and John, and he took over toughening them up. "I could not have told you this while he lived, but now all that is behind us," she said slowly. "When you were brought to me, though, he had come between me and Olivia and John. I needed your love desperately, and since you were not his daughter, Sam did not care if I spoiled you. You were all mine."

"Oh, I'm glad," I burst out.

She laughed.

"Since Sam had permitted me to keep you on condition that we all keep your coming to us a secret, I could not talk about it even with you," she said. "Yet after his death I could have told you, of course. I think I would have done if I had not discovered then that we were practically penniless. After we worked our way through that, we moved west and . . . and the right moment never seemed to come."

I took her hand and squeezed it and she smiled at me. Then she added, "I should have guessed that John would not wait, though, and I am so sorry."

By then, I knew almost everything I had wondered about.

I did not tell her that before I had started to ask her my questions, I had asked Olivia what she remembered about my coming to be her sister. She had looked at me and laughed.

"Oh, I was so jealous," she told me. "Father wasn't home and I thought I might get all Mother's attention with him away. Then Grandpa arrived with poor little you, wrapped up in a blanket and looking so pitiful. And Mother had no attention for an eight-year-old who could have been more help."

Olivia said she sat on her bed and sulked until Father came home. "And then it was too late to change my tune," she finished. "I'm sorry, little sister. Forgive me."

And of course I did. And now Mother was saying the same thing.

We were on our way back to Four Winds, hand in hand, when I decided to ask one more question.

"Is my birthday really in September?" I asked her.

"I didn't know for sure," she told me, reaching into her pocket. She pulled out a little drawstring bag and opened it. There was a ring inside it. She tipped it into my hand and went on.

"Ever since John confessed that he had broken his word, I've been carrying this ring with me. I knew the day must come that you would want to know more. I found this threaded on a cord around your neck. It was hidden from sight inside your dress. It's a sapphire, the September birthstone. Also, you had come to me on September first, so I chose that to be your birthday. It was as though your mother had sent me a message."

The ring was the most beautiful blue. I slid it onto my finger, but it was far too big.

"Do you remember her at all?" Mother asked softly.

I shook my head. I had tried ever since John told me the story of my being found. But no picture had come to me. I drew the beautiful ring off and tucked it back into the bag. Then I flung my arms around Mother's neck and hugged her with all my might. I could not speak. I had too big a lump in my throat.

Mother hugged me back. "Oh, Abby, are you angry at me for not being able to face life without you?" she said into my ear.

I was not, of course. I held on tight and let the tears flow. We were both growing very damp.

"Angry!" I got out at last. "How could I be angry? I love you with my whole heart. All I want is to be your Abby."

And I knew it was the truth.

Monday, May 11, 1903

When I told Bird that I had kept my promise, she was pleased with me, although she claimed she knew before I told her just by seeing the look on my face. I asked her to explain but she couldn't.

I do like having most of my story written down, even though the first chapter is lost. It is strange knowing that I must have had a different name once upon a time. And another birthday. Maybe I had brothers and sisters too. I will never know.

But I have decided not to brood about this. I don't want to be like John Thornley, constantly fretting about why this all happened.

Wednesday, May 13, 1903

Some people are leaving Frank. But not us. Anyway, we do not plan to leave. We will never be able to forget the night of the Slide, of course. We do still grieve for those we lost, but we have helped each other through the sorrow of it and now we are coming out of the shadow it cast, back into the sunlight. We think we will have people coming to the hotel just to see the devastation caused by the historic Frank Slide. We certainly still seem busy.

Some people who arrive climb up and stand on top of one of the boulders the landslide left behind. It's so huge they look like dolls. We have to travel around it to get by.

I have decided that sad memories are like that

massive rock. They wait to block our path. But we can get around them and go on past.

Monday, May 18, 1903

We hear that they are going to start mining again. I cannot believe it. But it is true. They say there is no danger of another landslide. I wonder what Bird's grandfather would say. Bird says he is like a ghost now. She thinks he feels he should have made people listen to his warnings.

Wednesday, May 20, 1903

Mother and I took my mother's ring over to the clockmaker's shop. He's a jeweller too. He says it will be easy to make the ring smaller to fit my finger. I can hardly wait to get it back and wear it.

Thursday, May 21, 1903

So much else has changed during the past weeks.

John has come to care more for us and to face the fact that Father was not the man he thought he was. He has also given up his job at the mine and is studying again to finish his high school subjects. Miss Wellington is tutoring him and Mother is so pleased about it. Miss Wellington says he should go to university. Mother said we had not the money, but Uncle Martin told her we would find it.

Although John was injured, and Jeremiah lost his leg, the people closest to me all survived. Polly seems to be recovering. Mother works with her at talking. It is not easy. But Polly does understand what Mother says even though she has to struggle to find words herself. She knows us all now and she is smiling again. The doctor says he thinks her memories will come back to her completely. She must not worry about this but just be patient.

I am nearing the end of this notebook. When I finish it, I will send it to Miss Radcliffe. She has promised to read it as soon as it gets to her, and send it back at once. All our letters back and forth fascinated her, she says. She wants to read every detail. She is so nice. I think she might be considering moving to Alberta. I hope she does. She says we are like her family.

I only have a few blank pages to fill now.

Friday, June 5, 1903

I know, I have not been writing much here. This afternoon I was just sitting gathering my thoughts when Connor's little sisters came racing into the hotel shouting for John. They had news. Charlie is alive! It took me a good two or three minutes to remember who Charlie was. But it wasn't a person. It is Charlie the horse, the one John used to take sugar cubes to during the winter.

They have dug into where his body was and found him. And, lo and behold, he is not dead at all!

John, still not fully recovered, jumped up and

hurried as fast as he could out the door to go see his old friend.

I wanted to go too but I had promised Mother to set the tables for supper, so I will have to go later. I cannot believe that blessed horse lived a whole month in the mine without food or water. I hope John comes straight home to tell us about how he is.

After supper

More sad news.

Charlie had chewed on his harness and on pieces of wood he found — that's what he ate inside the mine. He got water which had seeped in through cracks, I guess. John said he was terribly thin, just skin and bone. John got there in time to watch them making him a feast. They were so happy to find him alive that they made him a grand dinner of oats and barley and apples and brandy. He gobbled it down, and then he keeled over dead. They think it was too much for him. That much food all at once, after a month of near starvation, was more than his poor body could handle.

"He died happy, Abby," John said. But he had tears in his eyes when he said it.

Saturday, June 6, 1903

I keep thinking about Grandpa finding me on the dock. Mother says they thought I was not yet two, but later on she decided I was probably three because, when I at last started to speak, I knew lots of words and songs. I was weak, but when I grew strong I could walk and even run.

I am not nobody, as my poem said, but I will never know who I was before Grandpa found me. He'd asked people near where he found me if they knew anything about me, and other passengers were sure my whole family had died during the voyage, but nobody knew their names. The ship was crowded with people who were desperately ill. Once cholera broke out, so many perished and had to be buried at sea. In the confusion, records were not kept. It sounds as terrible as the Frank Slide.

Now I only have enough room left in my book to tell the last thing. I already wrote about Mother and me taking my ring to the jeweller to have it made smaller. Well, when we went to pick it up, something astonishing happened.

While Mother paid him, I slipped the ring on and held up my hand in a shaft of sunlight to see the stone sparkle. It caught the light and flashed a brilliant blue.

The jeweller smiled and said, "Whoever chose that ring must have spent time over it. It exactly matches the lassie's eyes."

Then Mother said, "I think it was chosen for her mother. It was far too big for a child's hand. I found it threaded on a cord around her neck, where her mother must have hung it for safekeeping. Perhaps she guessed she had not long to live."

I had not wondered why the ring was too large until that moment. I held up my hand again so that the sunlight would light up the stone once more before we had to leave.

And as I gazed into it, I found the face I thought I had lost.

It is hard to write about this. Maybe I should not try. It was only a glimpse. Then Mother took my elbow and steered me out of the shop. I stumbled on the doorsill but she steadied me. And when we reached the pavement, she said very gently, "What happened, Abby?"

"I remembered my mam's face," I whispered. "Her eyes were blue, exactly the same blue as mine."

"Oh, Abby," my mother breathed. Then she hugged me right there in front of the shop.

And we held hands all the way home.

Epilogue

—m—

Abby was unhappy about the mine opening again shortly after the landslide, but no disaster followed and a few years later, the original mine was closed.

As the people in Frank rebuilt their town and recovered from the shock of the landslide, Abby kept on with her busy life. The first blow she had to endure was the death of Davy when he was six. He got pneumonia, and this time his heart could not withstand the strain. In those days, there were no antibiotics to help fight such severe illnesses.

Davy's death left Abby grief stricken, but also freed her from having to care for him. It was a struggle for her to understand her confused feelings. It was hard for her to accept that it was normal for her to miss Davy and feel relief at the same time.

Connor and she went out together for a while, but they lost touch when his family moved to Lethbridge in 1907.

Martin Hill was involved in Alberta becoming a province in 1905, so involved that the work of running the hotel was left to the rest of the family. He had a heart attack in 1908 and, although he lived through it, he had another one a year later, which killed him.

Although Aunt Susan and Abby's mother still worked at managing the hotel, more and more of the responsibility fell to Mark. His girlfriend's family moved away from Frank after the Slide and, bit by bit after Connor left town, Mark and Abby drew closer. Finally they realized that, even though they had been raised to be cousins, they were not in fact related by blood. By the time Abby was in her late teens, they had grown close to each other and began to think about getting married. Abby's old teacher, Miss Radcliffe, had moved out west and she insisted Abby go on studying literature, which she loved. But when Abby was twenty, she and Mark did marry. The two of them took on the management of the hotel and cared for their mothers as they grew unable to carry the load.

Mark and Abby had four children, two girls and two boys. Abby was fearful that one of her babies might have the same problems as Davy, but the children were all healthy and a joy to their parents.

Bird married when she was just sixteen and, although she and Abby remained friends, Bird moved permanently to settle near Pincher Creek where her family lived. Before long the two young women were so busy raising their children and working in their communities that they did not see each other as often as they wished. Whenever they got a chance to get together, however, they picked up where they had left off and filled in all the gossip they had missed while they were apart. Bird named her only daughter Abby, and Abby named one of her girls Lark.

Olivia and Jeremiah had no children for several years, which was a disappointment to them; but then, much to their delight, Olivia got pregnant and they had a son whom they called John. Polly adored him and was a doting aunt. Olivia became a teacher and gave music lessons to Frank's children. She was also often asked to play at weddings and in concerts. Jeremiah got an artificial leg and taught himself to ride. Before long, he began to raise horses and give riding lessons. He took groups of young people on camping trips in the mountains and became a popular guide.

When John finished high school, for which he had to board in Pincher Creek, Miss Wellington encouraged him to go on to college and, with Uncle Martin's help, he became a doctor. He never married, although his sisters did their best to find him just the right girl. He volunteered for The Great War as a doctor in 1915 and was buried when a trench collapsed on him in 1917. He was rescued, but died later from his injuries.

Abby went on keeping a diary even when she was a busy mother and hotel manager. The story of how she was found by Grandpa Hill and brought to Mother became a family legend which was prized by all the children. Often they speculated on whom she might have been, but nobody ever learned the answer.

Historical Note

—⚭—

Frank, Alberta, is famous because of the massive rock slide that hurtled down Turtle Mountain and swept across the southeast edge of the town and up the other side of the valley. It occurred at 4:10 a.m. on Wednesday, April 29, 1903. Although the landslide lasted only 90 seconds and happened over a hundred years ago, Turtle Mountain today shows clear evidence of the devastation. The Slide left in its wake enormous boulders, some of which are still standing. Tall as houses, some rise up like giant tombstones, marking the place where the tragedy struck.

The town of Frank, in what was then the District of Alberta, North-West Territories, owes its origin to coal. In 1900 the Canadian American Coal and Coke Company began mining large deposits of coal from Turtle Mountain in the Crowsnest Pass. The coal was abundant, fairly easy to mine, and situated near the Canadian Pacific Railway tracks — convenient for shipping it out to buyers. A short mine spur connected the mine in Frank to the CPR.

Because of the coal mines and Frank's proximity to the Crowsnest Pass — a key route through the Rockies — the town attracted businessmen, tourists travelling through the pass, and of course, miners. By 1903 Frank had 600 inhabitants, served by an electrical plant and waterworks system, three hotels, well over a dozen businesses including a watchmaker, two restaurants, a bank, a post office, a school, a livery stable big enough to house fifty horses, a grocery store, a ladies' wear shop, a newspaper office and a Presbyterian Church.

Men had come from across North America, the British Isles, Scandinavia and Europe to explore the West and to work in the mines. Many were single, but quite a few brought their wives and children with them. When the people of Frank went to bed on that April night in 1903, nobody was fearful of a rock slide before sunrise, especially one that would come to be called the greatest landslide in Canadian history.

Unlike coal deposits in some other areas, the coal in Turtle Mountain was reasonably easy to mine. The mountain rose some 2300 metres above the town. Huge rooms, like caverns, were dug into the mountain. The tunnels were large and men could work standing up. Horses to pull the coal cars had ample room to move.

Tremors did happen fairly regularly, especially in the early morning hours, however. Small rockfalls, especially in the spring, were common. Nearby First Nations people kept their distance. They called Turtle Mountain "the mountain that moves," avoided the area, and would not work in the mine.

What caused the disastrous landslide of April 29, 1903? Over the years since, several reasons have been given. Perhaps the chief reason lay in the mountain's unstable geological structure. During its formation, layers of limestone were folded into a big A-frame shape. Further pressure opened up a crack in the earth's crust, a thrust fault, along which older layers of rock moved up and over younger ones. Other contributing factors were water freezing and thawing in summit cracks and coal mining at the mountain's base. Weather played a part too. Three of the four years before the Slide were unusually wet. In 1903 the snowpack was average, but a large amount of snow fell in March. The week before the Slide, it was unusually warm for several days and the melting snow filled the cracks. Then, on the night the Slide happened, the temperature dropped sharply, perhaps freezing water inside the fissures and increasing the internal pressure beyond the breaking point.

Early in the morning of April 29, 1903, a massive section of Turtle Mountain's eastern slope came crashing down. Some 82 million tonnes of limestone fell. Seventeen miners working the night shift were trapped in the mine. The mine entrance was buried. Miners' tents and cabins, as well as some of the town's houses and the livery stables, were crushed or buried. A 2-kilometre section of the CPR tracks was mangled under tonnes of rock. Fortunately, the Slide missed much of the town itself, including most of the commercial section. However, Old Man River, which ran near the town, was dammed up, became a lake and threatened to flood those parts of the town that had not been destroyed by the rock slide itself.

In the end, more than 90 people were killed and 23 injured. Among the dead were 21 children — some of them miners' children, others from the part of the town nearest the mine.

There were amazing stories of rescue or close calls, though. One teenager lived because she was staying overnight at the boarding house where she worked, but her entire family died — her mother and siblings in the house and her father outside the mine. One home was carried 6 metres off its foundation, but the family itself survived. Another family's home was horribly mangled, but the family members were unhurt. Seventeen trapped miners managed to dig their way out of the mine through a seam of coal, and after 13 hours emerged relatively unhurt. Three miners who had left the mine before their lunch break at 4 a.m., however, were not so fortunate. They were among the dead.

Amazingly, the mine reopened within weeks. The buried section of railway track was cleared and rebuilt. Later, a new mine entry was opened on the north side of the mountain, and a shaft was sunk in the valley.

Today visitors to the Crowsnest Pass gasp as they stare at the gigantic boulders. They visit the Frank Slide Interpretive Centre and are awestruck as they discover the stories of those who miraculously survived. They can also pause to see the graves of Gladys Ennis and her brother at the foot of Turtle Mountain.

Gladys was not yet two when the Slide buried her in mud. Her mother, sure she was dead, carried her body to a neighbour's house, where they cleaned her off and discovered she was in shock, but still alive. Gladys was the last survivor of the Slide; she died in 1995.

Dominion Avenue, one of Frank's main streets, housed shops, a bank, restaurants, a photography studio, a newspaper office and other businesses. The town had about 600 inhabitants at the time the Slide occured.

The Clark house, like so many others, was mangled by the boulders and stones that cascaded down Turtle Mountain on the night of the Slide.

The railway tracks lay buried, and Old Man River backed up to become a lake, endangering the town, until some of the debris was cleared. Since mining was the town's main industry, it was crucial to clear the tracks and keep the coal moving out as soon as possible.

Some of the massive boulders that fell were as large as houses.

After the Slide, the eastern face of Turtle Mountain lay exposed, with parts of the town still standing below it. This image, among many of the first photographs of the disaster, was taken by a local Frank photographer.

The Slide missed some of the town, but houses nearer the mine, and the miners' cabins, took the full brunt of the landslide.

International Morse Code

A •—	B —•••	C —•—•	D —••	E •	F ••—•
G ——•	H ••••	I ••	J •———	K —•—	L •—••
M ——	N —•	O ———	P •——•	Q ——•—	R •—•
S •••	T —	U ••—	V •••—	W •——	X —••—
Y —•——	Z ——••	0 (zero) —————	1 (one) •————	2 ••———	3 •••——
4 ••••—	5 •••••	6 —••••	7 ——•••	8 ———••	9 ————•

—— ——— •—• ••• • —•—• ——— —•• •

•• ••• •— ••• —•—— ••• — • ——

——— ••—• —•• ——— — ••• •— —• —••

—•• •— ••• •••• • •••

•—• • •——• •—• • ••• • —• — •• —• ——•

•—•• • — — • •—• ••• •— —• —••

—• ••— —— —••• • •—• •••

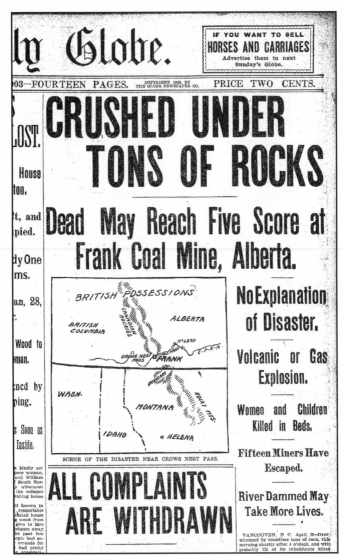

ly Globe.

03—FOURTEEN PAGES. COPYRIGHT, 1903, BY THE GLOBE NEWSPAPER CO. PRICE TWO CENTS.

CRUSHED UNDER TONS OF ROCKS

Dead May Reach Five Score at Frank Coal Mine, Alberta.

No Explanation of Disaster.

Volcanic or Gas Explosion.

Women and Children Killed in Beds.

Fifteen Miners Have Escaped.

River Dammed May Take More Lives.

VANCOUVER, B C, April 29—Over-whelmed by countless tons of rock, this morning shortly after 4 o'clock, and with probably 112 of its inhabitants killed

SCENE OF THE DISASTER NEAR CROWS NEST PASS.

ALL COMPLAINTS ARE WITHDRAWN

The Frank Slide made headlines around the world, including this front page from the April 30, 1903, Boston Daily Globe.

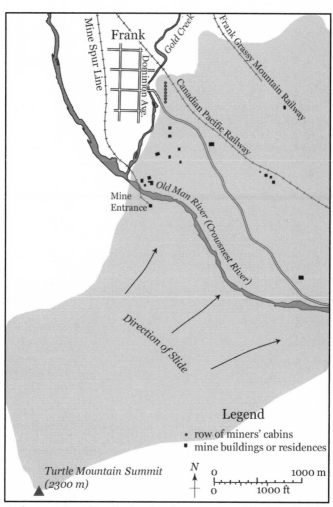

Mine Spur Line

Frank

Gold Creek

Frank Grassy Mountain Railway

Dominion Ave.

Canadian Pacific Railway

Mine Entrance

Old Man River (Crowsnest River)

Direction of Slide

Legend

• row of miners' cabins
■ mine buildings or residences

Turtle Mountain Summit (2300 m)

N

0   1000 m
0   1000 ft

A close-up view of Frank, showing the area covered by the rock slide, part of the town layout, and where the mine entrance and some houses and cabins lay buried. Gold Creek forged a new path on the west side of the slide debris and, due to constrictions, the river slowed and widened under Turtle Mountain.

Credits

—𝗺—

Cover cameo: © Samuel Schiff Co., N.Y.

Cover background: (detail) and page 187: View of Frank, Alberta, after the slide; Glenbow Archives NA-411-9.

Page 183: Dominion Avenue, Frank, Alberta; Marks and Buchanan, Glenbow Archives NA-414-2.

Page 184: Rescue team on site of Clark home, Glenbow Archives NA-586-2.

Page 185: Rebuilding railway to mine at Frank after slide, Glenbow Archives NA-672-3.

Page 186: Group on large rock at Frank Slide; Frank, Alberta; Marks and Buchanan, Glenbow Archives NA-3011-17.

Page 188: Remains of back row of cottages, after slide; Frank, Alberta; Glenbow Archives NA-3437-5.

Page 189: *Morse Code Chart*, from the website of the Canadian War Museum, courtesy of the Canadian War Museum.

Page 190: Front page from the *Boston Daily Globe*, April 30, 1903.

Page 191: Map © Paul Heersink/Paperglyphs.

The publisher wishes to thank Mr. R.L. Kennedy for providing information about the train schedule from Montreal to Frank; Barbara Hehner for her attention to the details; and Monica Field of the Frank Slide Interpretive Centre for sharing her encyclopedic knowledge of the Slide so generously. Thanks also to Dr. Bill Waiser for his expertise. Finally, thank you to Adria Lund and her team at the Glenbow Archives, who managed to provide images despite another disaster — the severe flooding in Calgary in July 2013.

This book is dedicated to Robert Heath,
my computer doctor
whose frequent house calls,
endless patience
and quick intelligence
have saved the lives of book after book.
It comes with my gratitude and deep affection.

Author's Note

One story which prompted this novel happened to a child in my own family. When a ship coming from Ireland docked in Canada, the disembarking passengers told of how cholera had broken out during the voyage, killing many of those who were emigrating to the New World. Among those who had survived was a small child whose identity nobody knew. In all the chaos on board that ship, this small girl was left with no one to claim her. She was brought home by a kind-hearted man whose family took her in while attempts were made to learn who she was. When this failed, she was adopted, given the name Elizabeth Egerton, and raised as a Canadian. Elizabeth grew up and married and became a distant relative of mine.

When I read about her in a book that told about our family tree, I was fascinated by the brief tale and longed to know more about what became of the child. Unable to find out any facts beyond the few notes in the book, I took what little I knew about Elizabeth and used it to create my heroine, Abby Roberts — hoping that Elizabeth, like my Abby, found happiness in Canada.

Another impetus for the story comes from my Aunt Jen's diary for 1889. I am fortunate that I come from a family where several people wrote diaries and kept old letters and told stories of things that had happened in years past. If my great-aunt had not done that, when she was twenty-four years old and she and her sister Gret decided to go out West to help their cousin Andrew run a hotel, Abby Roberts would never have been born, and certainly never have gone to Frank.

The diary is full of visits Jen and Gret made, dishes they washed, games they played and brief accounts of their meetings with young men. Nothing gives away the fact that both women met their future husbands during the months they spent in the West. Aunt Jen seldom sets down her feelings — which was wise of her, since it is clear that her sister often read what she wrote.

One entry I treasure is this: *We played tossing bean-bags last night. Gret cheated as usual.* Gret had written in tiny print up the margin that this is untrue.

Pages and pages are tedious, but every so often there is a funny bit or a surprising one. I was stunned by the entry reading: *This morning I got up early and made thirteen pies.*

Over and over, Jen speaks of the "sings." I only wish she had recorded the names of some of the songs. Many would have been hymns, I suspect, but I long to know more. Her relatives spent a good deal of time attending church services, prayer meetings and picnics. They went on visits that lasted several days, using a horse and buggy or gig or surrey or carriage or farm wagon to transport them. They also needed to be good at walking. And when they bought their groceries, they did not find everything in a supermarket, but went to several shops — the butcher, the baker, the grocer, the dairy, the feed store, the fish shop, the dry-goods store where they bought the cloth out of which they made clothing. Today it hardly crosses our minds as we buy ready-made outfits that the word "clothes" comes from the word "cloth."

If they got "stormstayed" during a visit, they settled down until the weather cleared. While visiting, the women helped with the housework and caught up on local news as they sewed or knitted or darned.

They played games and put on skits. There were no movies to go to, no television to watch, not even radio programs to listen to. They did have the telegraph, however, and both Aunt Jen and her sister Gret spent hours in the station working at "telegraphy." They must have learned the Morse Code, just as Abby did, and found sending and receiving telegrams fascinating.

Down Syndrome

Before I wrote Abby's story, a reader asked me about including a character with Down Syndrome in one of my books. That idea stayed with me and simmered for some time, but eventually took shape in *All Fall Down*, in the person of Abby's brother Davy.

In this story, Davy is born with a condition we now call Down Syndrome. At the time this story is set, he would have been known as a Mongoloid and would be called, by some people, a Mongolian Idiot. The name was given to such children because of an extra fold in their eyelids which makes them appear to slant. Down Syndrome results from a child being born with an extra copy of Chromosome 21. But in 1902 DNA had not yet been discovered, and nothing was known about chromosomes.

Often parents were urged to put such children into institutions, where they could be cared for until they died. After all, the doctors said, these children would never be able to walk or speak or learn, and probably would not live long. Many were born with heart defects, which shortened their lives.

Down children have other differences, including some or all of the following: They are smaller than other children and have shorter arms and legs, and stubby fingers and toes. Their faces can appear somewhat flat and their mouths and throats may be so small that feeding them is often difficult. They have trouble sucking on a nipple and frequently choke. Their ears are small and set lower than ears on other children. They are slow to develop both physically and mentally, but they are famous for their sunny dispositions when they are young.

In my story, Abby's love for her little brother enriches her life. Although caring for him is often burdensome, she cherishes him and recognizes, in him, a blessing she has been given.

During the writing of this book, I heard a scientist speak of the possibility of managing to engineer the chromosome that gives a child Down Syndrome in such a way that it will no longer cause abnormalities. She was quick to say that this is still far in the future. A young adult man with the syndrome, asked for his reaction to this, said he would be pleased to have some of his problems solved, but that he was reluctant to risk trying something that might alter his personality. As I listened to him and others, I thought about how complicated it is to be a human being with this particular set of challenges — not one, but a whole group of them. It is astounding that so much can be affected by one chromosome far too small to be seen by the naked eye.

About the Author

—◆◆—

All Fall Down is Jean Little's fifth title in the Dear Canada series. Her books have been read by generations of children. Some, such as *From Anna, Listen for the Singing, Mama's Going to Buy You a Mockingbird, Orphan at My Door* and *Pippin the Christmas Pig*, have become classics. Jean is a member of the Order of Canada and has won the Canada Council Children's Literature Prize, the CLA Book of the Year Award and numerous other awards, including the Matt Cohen Award: For a Writing Life.

Acknowledgements

—∾—

So many people helped make this story come to be.

First I owe thanks to my Great-aunt Jen and her sister, my grandmother, Gret. If they had not gone west in 1889 and if Aunt Jen had not kept a diary, Abby would never have existed.

My gratitude goes to my niece, Robin Little, who helped me with research.

My thanks go out to Sandra Bogart Johnston, my editor, for all her work, but most of all for her suggesting I set my new Dear Canada book in Alberta and include the Frank Slide.

As always, my deep gratitude goes to my sister Pat, who not only proofreads what I write, but tells me bits I should change or delete. She also persuades me to keep going every time I threaten to quit.

Pat also came with me on a pilgrimage to Frank, where I met Monica Field, the director of the Frank Slide Interpretive Centre. Monica read the manuscript and answered innumerable questions without complaining. Thanks to Monica and all the others in Frank and at the Centre who were welcoming and generous with information.

The staff at the Guelph Public Library and those at the CNIB Library also found answers to my many questions and supplied me with helpful books.

As usual, I owe deep gratitude, even though it is

sometimes grudging, to Barbara Hehner, who spots my many grievous errors and points them out. I long to argue, but she is always right.

I wish to thank Patsy Aldana and everyone else involved in my being given the Matt Cohen Award. The money paid for our trip to Frank and vastly enriched Abby's sense of place — she was not planning to mention weather until I felt the wind at Frank almost blow me over. Also, even though my vision is very limited, I gazed up at Turtle Mountain and felt its menace and beauty in a way no book had fully conveyed.

I found information on the Internet about Frank, but the two sources I turned to most often were: "The Frank Slide," by Frank Anderson, in *Triumph and Tragedy in the Crowsnest Pass*, ed. by Diana Wilson; and *Frank Slide* by J. William Kerr.

Copyright © 2014 by Jean Little

All rights reserved. Published by Scholastic Canada Ltd.
SCHOLASTIC and DEAR CANADA and logos are trademarks
and/or registered trademarks of Scholastic Inc.

www.scholastic.ca

Library and Archives Canada Cataloguing in Publication

Little, Jean, 1932-, author
All fall down : the landslide diary of Abby Roberts / by Jean Little.

(Dear Canada)
Issued in print and electronic formats.
ISBN 978-1-4431-1919-1 (bound).--ISBN 978-1-4431-2897-1 (html)

1. Landslides--Alberta--Frank--Juvenile fiction. I. Title.
II. Series: Dear Canada

PS8523.I77A64 2014   jC813'.54
                C2013-905323-9
                C2013-905324-7

6 5 4 3 2 1   Printed in Canada . 114   14 15 16 17 18

—ᴍ—

First printing January 2014

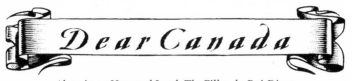

Alone in an Untamed Land, The Filles du Roi *Diary
of Hélène St. Onge* by Maxine Trottier

*Banished from Our Home, The Acadian Diary
of Angélique Richard* by Sharon Stewart

*Blood Upon Our Land, The North West Resistance Diary
of Josephine Bouvier* by Maxine Trottier

*Brothers Far from Home, The World War I Diary
of Eliza Bates* by Jean Little

A Christmas to Remember, Tales of Comfort and Joy

*A Country of Our Own, The Confederation Diary
of Rosie Dunn* by Karleen Bradford

*Days of Toil and Tears, The Child Labour Diary
of Flora Rutherford* by Sarah Ellis

*The Death of My Country, The Plains of Abraham Diary
of Geneviève Aubuchon* by Maxine Trottier

*A Desperate Road to Freedom, The Underground Railroad Diary
of Julia May Jackson* by Karleen Bradford

*Exiles from the War, The War Guests Diary
of Charlotte Mary Twiss* by Jean Little

*Footsteps in the Snow, The Red River Diary
of Isobel Scott* by Carol Matas

Hoping for Home, Stories of Arrival

*If I Die Before I Wake, The Flu Epidemic Diary
of Fiona Macgregor* by Jean Little

No Safe Harbour, The Halifax Explosion Diary
of Charlotte Blackburn by Julie Lawson

Turned Away, The World War II Diary
of Devorah Bernstein by Carol Matas

Where the River Takes Me, The Hudson's Bay Company Diary
of Jenna Sinclair by Julie Lawson

Whispers of War, The War of 1812 Diary
of Susannah Merritt by Kit Pearson

Winter of Peril, The Newfoundland Diary
of Sophie Loveridge by Jan Andrews

With Nothing But Our Courage, The Loyalist Diary
of Mary MacDonald by Karleen Bradford

Go to www.scholastic.ca/dearcanada for information on the Dear
Canada series — see inside the books, read an excerpt
or a review, post a review, and more.